The White Apache Returns Home

By
Ralph Gatlin

PublishAmerica
Baltimore

First printing

All characters in this book are fictitious, and any resemblance to real persons, living or dead, is coincidental.

PublishAmerica has allowed this work to remain exactly as the author intended, verbatim, without editorial input.

ISBN: 1-60672-146-1
PUBLISHED BY PUBLISHAMERICA, LLLP
www.publishamerica.com
Baltimore

Printed in the United States of America

The White Apache Returns Home

This book is dedicated to my family and our special friends. This is also dedicated to the people we know that have Parkinsons, Multiple Sclerosis, Strokes, Cancer or other problems. They are special, courageous people. The path of life God (Ussen) leads each of us on is not always an easy one to travel.

Prologue

The West was in turmoil in 1868. The settlers and the Indians were in a war that would decide who would remain on the land called "The New Mexico Territory." The Territory was composed of parts of what is now Arizona, New Mexico, Texas, and the mountains of northern Mexico. I was captured and lived with the Apaches in that territory for ten years. I became an Apache. I married White Fawn. She was expecting a baby in three months when the Comanche raided Victorio's village. Thirty-four warriors and I were off on our winter hunt. White Fawn and many Apaches were killed just hours before we returned. I took ten warriors and went after the Comanche. We caught them in a deep ravine they had taken as shelter from the bitter winter storm. Only six Comanche survived.

We got revenge for the dead and wounded, but it was obvious that it was the beginning of the end for Victorio and his Apaches. The bad times got worse. I lost more friends to the enemies of the Apache. Victorio's tribe was almost decimated. The Apaches and the Shaman believed a big strike against the settlers would make them leave the land of the Apaches and bring back the good times. Nana was chosen to lead a raid on Tucson. Since Victorio and I voted against it, we would not go on it.

Ussen came to me in a dream. He told me it was time for me go back home to my real father's ranch. Ussen also told me to warn the people of Tucson of the impending raid lead by Nana. I left the Apaches. It is treason to the Apaches and punishable by death. Victorio, Chato and Nana have been after me three days. They have me trapped in a small valley 400 miles from Tucson.A terrible noise north of me made me think of the time when Victorio told me of the day when the earth trembled and the terrible sound it made as the earth opened up to make great canyons. Victorio had told me the story word for word just like his father had told him and his father had told him. The ground trembles under my feet. The noise gets louder in the northern part of the valley. I can't believe my eyes. I see what may be the last big herd of buffalo in America. They are stampeding. Sizzling bolts of lightning burn their way through the sky, striking the ground all around the buffalo. The lightning makes them crazy with fear. They begin to run as fast as they can to get away from it.

I make my decision. I gather my weapons and run down into the valley in front of the stampeding buffalo. It doesn't look good for me. I am almost in a trance. I stop thinking. I let my instincts take over. I envision myself flying just above the buffalo, looking down on them. It is easy to see that I won't make it. I am lucky that I have come out at the valley's narrowest point. It might not make any difference. A boulder juts out from the other side. It looks like I will be about ten yards short of the boulder when the herd gets to me. Everything seems to go into slow motion. I try to run faster. The buffalo are closing in on me. I am not going to make it. The big, shaggy buffalo leading the herd has his head down and coming straight at me. The buffalo are wall to wall in the valley. There is no way out. If this is Ussen's way for me to die I am ready. The big buffalo leading the herd steps into a prairie dog hole, breaking his right leg. He turns a flip going end over end. Others fall over him causing the buffalo behind them to try and swerve around them. Nothing can stop the crazed herd as they run over the buffalo that are down. The downed buffalo become a part of the valley floor.

It does slow the others down a little. It gives me just enough time to dive behind the boulder. Victorio is holding his breath. He relaxes when he sees me dive behind the boulder. He thinks, "It is a good thing that Ussen has other plans for my son, Lone Eagle. Ussen acts in mysterious ways sometimes."

I scramble up the boulder and hold my bow up so Victorio, Chato and Nana could see me. They do the same. It is a sign of respect.

The wind, that always precedes a bad storm, brings great gusts of rain mixed with hail in slanting sheets of water. Lightning bolts continue to light up the sky. Thunder rumbles down the valley causing the buffalo to run faster. The rain and hail knock the dust down but they also block my vision of the three Apaches on the other side of the valley. I am safe now. I still must go to Tucson and warn them of the impending raid by the Apaches. Then I must go back to my real home.

This book is about my long journey home and the end of life's journey for Victorio and Morning Star. This story is fiction but it could have been true.

Chapter One

I am alone again. This time I am truly alone. I am caught between two worlds. One is the world of the settlers and the other is the world of the Apaches. I am a part of both worlds. Yet I am neither fully an Apache, nor a settler. It is not like it was when Victorio captured me ten years ago. This time I'm not afraid when I wake up. I am nineteen years old and almost 6 feet tall. I weigh about 180 pounds. I am caught between two ways of life. I was nine years old when Victorio captured me. He and Morning Star adopted me after one year. Since then I have become an Apache. I get under the over hang of the boulder to get away from the rain and hail hitting the ground all around me. I look carefully to make sure one of the big rattlesnakes is not sharing the overhang with me. Before I go to sleep I use my shirt to catch enough water to fill my water bag. I sleep for an hour until the storm passes. The overhang has kept me dry, and protected from the hail, rain, and the strong wind blowing in on me. I have caught enough water to last at least two more days.

The buffalo herd still fills the valley, blocking the Apaches when I leave. I am safe now. I will go on and warn the people of Tucson even though I know the Apaches will not make the raid on them because it will no longer be a surprise. They will not attack if they think many of their warriors would be killed. Victorio's Apaches are fighting a defensive war now. One they can't win. I drink a little water from my deerskin bag and start my 400-mile journey to Tucson and then to the ranch of my father.

I glance back the way I have come. I am leaving a lot of good memories and people I love behind. I would have stayed with the Apaches if White Fawn had lived and Ussen had allowed me to.

I start my journey toward Tucson. I am careful not to leave too many tracks. I stay on the cap rock as much as I can. I brush my tracks away when I cross an obvious trail. I travel next to the shadows just under the ridges of the foothills for the next six days. One of those days I saw an Army patrol way out in the distance. A smaller dust cloud trailed some distance behind them. It was probably made from a small war party of Indians trailing the troopers, hoping they will make a mistake. Things have changed. It is the Calvary that controls the land now. It is they who come and go as they please.I move out in a brisk trot. I travel mostly after the heat of the day is over and I run until it begins to get light and then again as the sun completes its journey into its resting place. I stop briefly at a place in the rocks where there is a spring. The water seeps through the rocks and disappears into the sand. Only the Apaches know about this spring. It takes me a while to make a catch basin that holds enough water to fill my water bag. I catch a large lizard. I don't think it is poisonous but when I cut its head off I made sure I removed the sacs that held the poison. I didn't want the poison coming out on the meat. It wouldn't kill me but it would make me sick. It is a good meal for me. I do not travel after the sun has begun its journey across the sky. I find a place that shelters me from the sun for as long as I need to stay there. I consume less water this way and I sometime find something to eat that is also hiding from the sun. The hot sun will cure the meat from the lizard in about three hours.

It is the morning of the eighth day on my journey. I am in no particular hurry. I am enjoying my freedom. I am alert to any movement, any change in the sounds around me. I still have special feelings for this semi-desert land. The night before had brought me a vision. It is a long time in the future. I saw Indians, settlers and blue coats all sitting at the same table. All of them are treated as equals. Victorio will never know this but one day all men may live together as brothers. It will be a long time coming. No one living today will be there to see it. The Apaches will be treated with the same respect all the others are. It is good to see this.

I have seen some signs of Indians and soldiers but the signs are several days old. I am glad no one has seen me. I remember the many times in the past I have spent days traveling looking over the picturesque countryside. The red rock formations form shapes that make you wonder if Ussen is leaving us a message. The rocks are sculptured by the wind and rain over a period of millions of years. They are beautiful.

I have never been this far west. I am glad that I haven't seen any one in the last few days. I know if an army patrol spots me they will shoot me on sight. So will the Navajo. So will the Apaches. I look more like an Apache than Nana does. The Navajo would love to kill me, "Lone Eagle, son of Victorio." Any settler that sees me will see me as an Apache and try to kill me. I have no friends. I have yet to make a decision what my new life will be.I have traveled only a few miles when I smell the smoke of a campfire. It has to be a trap or a greenhorn. All of the Indian Tribes use campfires to attract their enemies. After going a mile more down the trail I can see where the smoke is coming from. I cover the last 300 yards with extreme caution. It is as I suspected. It is a blue coat. He has made a pot of coffee. The campfire is built on a sandy knoll. The brush grows right up to the edge of his camp.

I know a lot about the trooper already. I know he is a greenhorn and he has been lucky up to now. I know he won't live long out here unless he gets smarter. He is one day out of Tucson. This means he has already used up most of his luck. I have the sensation on the back of my neck that means something is wrong. It is not the blue coat. Some one else is nearby. All of my senses become alert. The trooper has let his coffee cool too much. He can't stand coffee that is not hot. He throws it out and pours himself another cup. After blowing on the lip of the cup he takes a swallow. He sets down his cup and stands up. He has his suspenders off his shoulder so he can tuck his shirt in. He pulled up his suspenders. He takes the yellow bandana he used to pick up the hot coffee pot and ties it around his neck. My senses are going full blast. Something bad is about to happen. I start to warn him. I am too late.

He still had his arms up when an arrow comes flying out of the brush hitting him in his chest and spinning him around. A second arrow knocks him into the fire. He jars the coffee pot, almost knocking it over. I felt sorry about his death. I would like to have warned him but I might have had to kill him myself when I made myself known to him. Right now I don't know how I feel about soldiers or Indians but I do know how they feel about me! The only ones I really know and trust are Victorio and his Apaches and my real family. They are the only ones I can totally trust. It seemed to me that I am faced with a lot of enemies on both sides because I am different. Ussen has told me it is right for me to be different and that I will have to fight sometimes because I am different.

The mesquite, sage, cactus and tumbleweeds keep the Navajo from spotting me.

If the Navajo don't see me I will slip away and go on to Tucson. I can do nothing to help the trooper. I still wonder why the blue coat had not sensed the Navajo. Why didn't the Navajo feel my presence? I watched three Navajo bound out of the brush, whooping and hollering. They run over, pull the soldier out of the fire and scalp him. The three young braves acted like they had just wiped out a Regiment of Calvary instead of ambushing one unsuspecting greenhorn. They opened the trooper's saddlebags, throwing out papers and a white shirt. The smallest of the three Navajo put the shirt on. It almost swallowed him, hanging down to his knees. The other two laugh loudly. They are having a good time with the dead soldier's belongings. One Navajo, obviously the leader, picked up the metal coffee cup, poured himself a half-cup of coffee and took a big swallow, burning his lip and tongue. The coffee tasted so bad that he spit it half way across the clearing. He turned and threw the remaining coffee and the cup into the fire. Then he kicked the coffee pot over. One Navajo found a pair of woolen socks in the saddlebags and put them on his hands. The leader took the trooper's sidearm, belt and holster. The holster was burned a little bit.I watched this from my hiding place making sure no other Navajo were out in the brush. The leader of the Navajo sent the smaller and youngest brave after their horses. I got ready, if they were going to sense my presence it would be soon. I took six arrows out, holding five in my left hand. I notched the sixth one. The leader must have felt me looking at him. He turned and looked directly at me. He began to yell and tried to get one of his arrows out. I shot him in his chest. The other Navajo spun round facing where the sound of the bowstring came from. He too tried to get an arrow out. He was slow, too slow, and paid for his carelessness. The smallest brave was not a coward. He let the horses he was holding go and charged me trying to ride over me. My arrow plucked him off his horse only a few feet from me. The brave got off one arrow that barely missed me. The Navajo bounced heavily on the ground, driving my arrow deeper into him. He tried to get up so I shot him again. He was a brave, young warrior.The fight lasted less than a minute. I pulled the smoldering saddlebags out of the fire, putting sand on them. I put the papers back in the unburned side of the saddlebags. I gathered up their old guns, pulled out all of my arrows except the one that had broken when the Navajo fell on it. I put two of their arrows with mine.I loaded the dead trooper on his horse, and after thinking on it for a few seconds I put one of the dead Navajo on his horse also. I didn't want the people of Tucson to think I had shot the trooper. I started to put on the dead troopers burnt clothes but they didn't fit. I didn't like the idea anyway. I found a food pouch on one of the Navajo. I ate all of the dried deer meat he had in it. The Apaches put berries and nuts in their pemmican and it tastes better. I kicked sand on the campfire and rode out. I wondered how I would be accepted when I rode into Tucson, only a day away. Buzzards started flying circles above me after the bodies had been on the horses a couple of hours. The horses I had tied together were getting nervous about the smell and the buzzards. The bodies bloated in the hot sun and smelled so bad I was tempted to leave them and let someone in the Army come back and get the trooper's body if they wanted to. I only had a short distance to go so I decided to take the bodies on in with me. I keep my eyes moving making sure we were not riding into a trap. It's probably a good thing I did. The vultures circling overhead were a dead give a way. It turned out I didn't have to go into Tucson. The tenth Calvary is camped by the Sabine River a few miles NE of Tucson. It had water in it now but sometimes in the summertime it would dry up. Water was the controlling factor on where you lived in the west.I stopped a hundred yards from the sentry holding my palm out in the universal sign of peace. The sentry got excited and called for the Sergeant of the Guard. Other blue coats started coming out of their tents. All of them turned up their noses at the smell coming from the bodies. They began to get excited. A few went back for their guns. I walked slowly up to the sentry.I heard someone come up behind me. A big hand spun me around and a fist knocks me down. It stunned me but it also made me mad. He reaches down to snatch me off the ground. I already had my Bowie Knife coming out of its sheath and I would have gutted him in a second or two.

A voice of authority stopped both of us. It saved Sergeant Butch Gaston's life and mine also. Of course the troopers would have killed me after I killed him.

It was the voice of Lieutenant Lin Miller. He was a good officer, respected by his superiors and the men under him. I explained to the

Lieutenant in halting English how I had seen the Navajo kill the trooper called Ed Wales. I had heard the men around me whispering the dead soldier's name. The Lieutenant looked closer at me. At first he had thought I was an Apache. Now he thought me to be worse, a white man turned Apache, a renegade. I started to tell him of my capture by Victorio ten years ago. The Lieutenant stopped me. He noticed that his troopers were getting worked up because of the death of trooper Wales. He told one of the bystanders. "Take these horses over to the corral." He told another one, "Take care of the Navajo's and Trooper Wale's bodies. Bring his dispatches to me." He sent all the others to their tents. He told Sergeant Gaston, "Take this man to my tent, I'll be with you in a few minutes." Sergeant Gaston took me over to the Lieutenant's tent, keeping his eyes on me all the way. He had been surprised when I had come off the ground so quickly after he hit me. No man had ever taken his best punch before and got up. He stood a couple of inches taller than me. He outweighed me by at least twenty pounds. Lieutenant Miller came into the tent holding the papers that had been in the saddlebags of Trooper Wales. Lieutenant Miller asked me. "What happened to Trooper Wales?" I told him that Trooper Wales knew nothing of staying alive in Indian Territory. At first Sergeant Gaston bristled. He shook his head several times. His respect for Lieutenant Miller was all that kept him from losing control and coming after me. At first my English was hesitant. Occasionally I used an Apache word instead of English.

Soon both he and Lieutenant Miller believed me. I told them of my capture and of my ten years as an Apache and of being Victorio's son. I didn't tell it trying to get either sympathy or praise. It was just the way that it was. I mentioned to them about the raid the Apaches had planned on Tucson and that they would not attack now. They could tell that I admired and respected Victorio and his Apaches. When I finished my story, Sergeant Gaston and Lieutenant Miller shook hands with me. Sergeant Gaston told me, "I'm sorry I let my temper get the best of me. I was upset because of Trooper Wales. None of these men know anything about fighting Indians. A lot more of them will be killed before it's over."

It made Lieutenant Miller start thinking. "Who could teach them how to fight Indians and survive in the desert better than a man who has lived with and was trained by the Apaches?" Lieutenant Miller looked closely at me. I looked bigger than my 5 feet eleven inches. My brown skin and my dark hair resembled the Apaches. I did not tell them that I was "Lone Eagle-The White Apache." Only my eyes were different from the dark eyes of the Apaches. They were brown, almost tawny with small yellow flecks in them. Not like the black, flat, dead eyes of the Apaches.The Lieutenant shuddered a little as he looked at me and thought, "I'm glad he's on our side. He kind of gives me the willies." He didn't know that right now I didn't have a side. I was still trying to figure it out. Since I had my shirt off they could see the puckered holes of a couple of bullet wounds and a thin purple line that ran from my chest down to below my belly button. I was dressed in a breechcloth, knee length moccasins and a headband. One man had come awful close to gutting me. Lieutenant Miller asked me, "What are your plans?" I told him. "I'm going back to see about my family. They live east of here, not too far from Santa Fe. The Lieutenant said, "Santa Fe is over 400 miles away."

I told him, "Their ranch is about sixty miles north-west of Santa Fe."

"This isn't much but it will help you some." Sergeant Gaston reached into his pocket and pulled out a ten-dollar bill.

"I don't need the money, I can always find enough to eat." Lieutenant Miller shook his head. "It's different now, you won't be living as an Indian anymore, you are going to need some money. I've got a proposition for you."He continued. "I have eighty four men in this outfit. Only a few of us have ever fought anyone, much less Indians. I hope you will train them so they will have a chance when we do fight." I thought about it a minute. I was ready to go home, but I had been gone ten years; one more month would not hurt me. I told

Lieutenant Miller, "I will help train your men for one full moon." We didn't discuss the amount of money I would be paid. Lieutenant Miller told me. "You will have an easier time if you have your hair cut and you dress more like us. I have an old shirt, boots and a pair of pants you can use. You are about the same size as I am."

Sergeant Gaston told me. "I'll go get the company barber while you are taking a shower."Lieutenant Miller asked Private Jody Bates to show me where the shower was. A fifty-five gallon drum had been placed on a seven-foot platform. A hole in the bottom of it had a plug in it. You pulled the plug to release the water. I wondered why they didn't just use the river to bathe in. I found out most of them didn't take baths regularly. The one using it had to refill it from the river anyway. I was given a bar of lye soap that smelled terrible. I thought, "No wonder the white eyes stink so much." I decided to try it one time. By the time I had finished my bath any Apache could smell me a long way off. They could find me quickly. I finished my shower and put on the Lieutenants clothes, all but the boots. They were too hard, uncomfortable, and stiff for me. I put my moccasins back on. Private Bates refilled the barrel for me. The barber was waiting, along with Sergeant Gaston and Lieutenant Miller when I got back to the Lieutenant's tent. I would only let the barber cut off part of my hair. I thought of how my Comanche enemies would like to have a chance to cut my hair and my throat. I had no facial hair. Each hair that had grown earlier had been plucked out by its roots as the Apaches did. The face that looked back at me from the barber's mirror was not familiar to me. It shocked me that I didn't look much like an Apache now. I didn't look like a settler either. I felt kind of funny. I looked just like I felt, neither a settler nor an Apache.Sergeant Gaston had the Quartermaster issue me two blankets, two sheets, a pillow, canteen and a small tent. The bugler was blowing taps as he finished giving me the stuff. Lieutenant Miller told me he would buy the three Navajo horses I brought in. It would give me some money while I was in camp. Sergeant Gaston and Lieutenant Miller took me to the Mess Hall for the evening meal. I found out why Army Dining Halls are called Mess Halls. We were served red kidney beans, a hard biscuit, a kind of unidentifiable dark meat in a watery gravy, and potatoes that were quite good. I had no trouble eating with the knife and fork even though it had been a long time since I had used them. Every thing seemed to be coming back easy now. I figured I would fix my own supper after this. I tried it but I didn't like the strong, steaming hot coffee even though I almost filled my cup with sugar. We created quite a stir when we walked into the Mess Hall. I walked on my insteps while the troopers walked almost flatfooted. That explained why the Apaches could run them down if they were on foot. The ones who had seen me ride into the camp were amazed by the difference in the way I looked now. There was no doubt now that I was white. Most of the men in the Mess Hall smiled when they saw me, others frowned. Most of the sentiment had switched over to me now that every one had a chance to think about it and to see me. My surviving the ten years with the Apaches made them think better of me. One man in the Mess Hall didn't like me. He had no reason to dislike me. He didn't even know me. He had no experience with me. In fact he had never said a word to me.

Chapter Two

Ron Jedrokoski didn't need a reason to dislike someone. It came automatically to him. Especially when he was drunk or just feeling mean. He was the bully of the outfit. Private Ron Jedrokoski enlisted in New York City. Rumor had it that he had enlisted rather than go to jail. He gave out an aura of hate. He was a shade over six feet, three inches. He weighed something over 250 pounds, none of it fat. He had several of his cronies around him, men he intimidated and used.Jedrokoski's parents came from Poland, expecting to find that America was a paradise. They settled in New York. Petrov Jedrokoski got a job loading and unloading ships in the harbor. Ron was born a year later. Times got better for them. It was much better than Poland had been. When Ron was eight years old an influenza epidemic swept through New York killing over a hundred thousand people. Ron's parents were the first to go. He got terribly sick. He spent eight days shivering, burning up with fever. He stayed in the beat up old shack his family had lived in. Abe Bellows, who lived in the shack next to the Jedrokoskis, had some kind of natural immunity and didn't catch the flu. He came by and saw that Ron's parents were dead. He put them in the death wagon that came through the neighborhood regularly. He fed Ron occasional bowls of soup, gave him water and watched him until he finally got well. He didn't do it because he liked Ron. He did it because he had a use for him. Ron lost twelve of his eighty pounds in the eight days he was sick. Abe gave Ron one day more to recuperate and then sent him out to steal off the docks like the four other boys he had working for him. Ron got beat up by the boys who were bigger and meaner than he was. He came back empty handed. He got a worse beating by Abe. He had to go back and steal something of value. He did.He learned something with each beating and by the time he was thirteen years old he was big enough and mean enough to be the one giving the beatings. He became the boss of the smaller boys who were stealing off the docks.Abe Bellows continued taking most of the money Ron made stealing. He beat Ron ever so often just to teach him a lesson. One day he made a mistake. Ron was fifteen. Abe was drunk when he jumped on Ron. Ron had waited years for that moment. Abe thought he had Ron so afraid of him that he didn't have to worry about him. Abe continued drinking. Ron waited until Abe passed out. He got his knife out, the long one that Abe had never seen. He placed the point over Abe's heart and rammed it home. He became the king of the docks.Abe's body was never found. Ron was free, at least for eight years. Ron's reputation for toughness and meanness grew. He loved to fight. He loved to dish out punishment. He could take it too. One day he went too far. During a brawl on the docks he killed a man, the son of a rich man. The police didn't try to prove any thing. They were tired of him. They arrested him. The judge gave him an option; ten years in prison or he could enlist in the Army.He was transferred West after getting in trouble several times in his barracks in New Jersey. He had two years left on his enlistment. He had respect only for the strong such as Sergeant Gaston and Lieutenant. Miller. They both earned his respect. It had held him in check for the six months he had been part of the 10th Calvary. He controlled the poker games in the camp. He had connections in town that got him booze and women. Rumor was that

Black Jack Ketchum was his contact in town. Ron had a place to sell the merchandise he stole from the troopers and the government. A lot of troopers knew this but none of them would tell on him. They were afraid of him and rightfully so.Sergeant Gaston suspected him and had informed Lieutenant Miller. They had not caught him stealing so far.Jedrokoski's eyes narrowed as we walked into the mess hall. We talked for a long time that evening. Lieutenant Miller agreed to pay me thirty-one dollars for the month of training. I could sleep in camp and eat with the Army. In addition Lieutenant Miller bought the three Indian horses for twenty-two dollars a piece. I would be issued a new seventeen shot Winchester to use as long as I trained the troopers. I agreed to all of this. I knew nothing of the value of money but I trusted the Lieutenant.That night I moved my blankets outside the tent issued me. The cot was terrible. The small tent made me feel closed in and made me wish for the open skies. The sentry making the rounds watched me carefully as I pulled the blanket around me. He still didn't trust me completely. I was up and already through bathing in the river when the bugler woke the troopers up. I was walking back to my tent when I heard someone say something to bait me.The voice was not speaking to me but about me. Ron Jedrokoski sat on one of the empty powder kegs. He looked at me when he said, "Look at that murdering Apache. I bet he turned his own mother over to the Apaches to save his worthless hide. I bet he smiled as he watched what they done to her." I stopped, considering the best thing to do. Jedrokoski, who was enjoying himself continued on. "I bet he's a coward too. He sure looks like one." All of the men around him laughed at his remarks. I walked toward the small group of men. I looked Jedrokoski over.He had a barrel chest, black hair all over him. His nose was flat. Part of one ear was gone. He had a scar over one eye. His eyes were small and mean. I could sense the evil in the man. I told him, "You are like the Wolverine, who does not kill to eat but kills because he loves killing. You wish to destroy everything around you. One day your evil will destroy you." Jedrokoski grunted; I had responded enough to justify him fighting me. He would be able to kill or cripple me and get away with it. He had to be careful. He wanted to stay in the Army the rest of his enlistment.He was off the empty powder keg like a shot. Being much heavier than I was he planned to bowl me over, and stomp me while I was down. I was a little surprised at the speed and agility shown by him. I stepped aside at the last second, lashed out with my foot catching him on the side of his knee. I used only enough force to hurt him, not to cripple him. He was a little off balance, favoring his knee a little. He rushed me again. I grabbed his arm, used his momentum to throw him over my shoulder. He hit the ground heavily. He raised his hands over his head and face, expecting me to put the boots to him. He knew he would have done it to me. I stood back, waiting for him to get up. He looked up in surprise. Ron thought, "What a dummy, I would have ended the fight right then." He got up. He knew he had three choices. He could fight a little more and quit, acting like he had enough. He could fight until one of us got seriously hurt, or killed, or he could back down. He couldn't back down. No one would respect him after that. He really didn't have a choice. He had to fight until he crippled me so bad I couldn't fight. Then he would kill me. He approached me slowly. He would take his time, and enjoy very minute of it. All he needed to do was to get me in his bear hug one time. He would squeeze me until I cried out for mercy. He had broken the backs of two miners in fights in the Wild Horse Saloon in town. The miners had wound up screaming for mercy, asking him to stop. He didn't give them any. One of them might walk again, the other wouldn't. At first Jedrokoski paid no attention to the punches I kept throwing at his face. He hit me once, knocking me six feet through the air. I had caught the punch on my arms. It had numbed both of them for a few seconds. I was up before he could get to me.His face began to turn beet red. The scar above his eye burst open. He looked a lot worse off than he was. I got caught by one of those big fists on the side of my head. Stars exploded all around me. I couldn't see for a second or two. Jedrokoski shuffled toward me, smiling now. It was his fight. He looked up expecting to see fear in my eyes. The flat confident look I had in my eyes made him grunt. He reached for me. He gave a gasp when I ripped a hard right into his belly. I followed it up with a couple more. For the first time Jedrokoski realized he was getting a little tired. He also had begun to feel the punches. He still wasn't hurt much. I had no idea how long we had fought. He hit me a few times but he had not hurt me with any of them except the two times. His right eye was swollen shut. His lip was split. Blood trickled out of his nose. His stomach was red all over. He had a pain in his side and his arms were getting heavy. I had a black eye surrounded by a red circle of bruised flesh. My arms and shoulders were sore. Red places were evident everywhere he had hit me. Otherwise I was not hurt much. The ones watching the fight thought Ron would soon kill me easily. The tide was changing. I was still fresh. He was beginning to take deep breaths. Some of them were pulling for me now. The four cronies of Jedrokoski backed up and had gotten quiet. I moved back a little. I caught my leg on the rope holding a tent pole and almost fell. Jedrokoski had his chance. He tried to grab me several times during the fight only to run into a stiff right or left. He moved forward, grabbed me as I regained my balance. He got me in his bear hug. My feet were off the ground. He ignored the rain of blows on him. I still had my arms free.Jedrokoski tucked his chin into my chest, gradually increasing the pressure. He knew the fight was almost over. I felt my ribs start to grind together. I opened my hands, cupped them, and hit his ears as hard as I could. Shock waves went all through him. The pressure of the air forced into his eardrums ruptured them. He relaxed his hold on me. The pressure eased up on me for a second. It was enough. I grabbed his head, brought my own forehead down on the bridge of his nose, shattering it. Blood splattered all over us. He stepped back. He dropped me. He was almost blind by the pain and the blood from his nose. Tears poured from his eyes. I hit him on his nose again. Jedrokoski shook his head. He was not through yet. A great rage consumed him. He started swinging his massive fists as fast as he could. One of them caught me on the side of my head. Again the stars flashed before my eyes. I didn't go down this time. I shook my head to clear it. He stalked me now, carefully looking for the one opening where he could end it.He made an effort to kick my legs out from under me. I retaliated, catching the side of his knee with my foot. Everyone around us heard the pop as the cartilage tore in his knee. He was beyond feeling pain now as he shuffled forward, keeping as much weight off his right leg as he could. I got hit again. This time it had no effect on me. I was caught up in the heat of the fight. I could see that he was not going to quit. Something in him was twisted. He fought because he loved to inflict pain. He would have to be taught that he too could be hurt. I began to methodically beat him on his face, ribs, stomach and chest. It was almost like I was cutting down a tree. My left caught him on the nose. It stopped him in his tracks. A low moan came out of him now. He began swinging his head back and forth as he came forward. The troopers had never seen anything like this fight. A stinging right caught Ron on his ear. My left thundered into his stomach. A right to his heart and another left to his nose. He stood dead still, shaking his head back and forth, as I continued to punish him. There was no pity in me. I had seen men like him before. They used their size to beat and humiliate the weaker ones around them. They were mavericks, one of a kind. If they were channeled right they became famous men. If not, you had to kill them to get rid of them. They would not quit. It was time for me to finish this. Sergeant Gaston and Lieutenant Miller walked up. Sergeant Gaston started to intervene. Lieutenant Miller stopped him saying, "It looks like Private Jedrokoski is getting a lesson in fighting. He has needed it for some time." Sergeant Gaston had figured that sooner or later he was going to have to fight Jedrokoski. He had not felt entirely sure that he could beat him. He watched as I continued working on him. Ron was having trouble breathing. The blood from his shattered nose ran down his throat choking him. A blow to his throat had created partial paralysis. Both eyes were swollen shut. Blood ran from his ears. His eyes were beginning to glaze. He still would not quit. I hit him in his rib cage with my right. He did not seem to be aware of the punch. He began to use his fists again, although much slower now. I didn't even bother ducking them. They had no steam to them.I measured Jedrokoski, brought a right hand all the way up from the floor, catching him flush on his chin. He had his mouth open, trying to get as much air in his lungs as he could. His broken nose allowed no air through it. It was totally useless now. Jedrokoski's jaws snapped together, breaking his bottom jaw. He was out on his feet. I started to hit him again. He wobbled. Then he slowly fell forward, landing hard on his face. He quivered once and lay still.The Army Doctor stepped forward. He asked for 4 volunteers to carry Jedrokoski to the base hospital tent. No one volunteered. He was disliked that much. Lieutenant Miller talked with Doctor Conrad a minute, then ordered four men to carry Jedrokoski to the Doctor's tent. Doctor Bob Conrad requested that Lieutenant Miller send a man to Tucson to get the town Doctor. It seems that Jedrokoski was going to need a lot of medical work done on him. Everyone crowded around me clapping me on the back. Beating Jedrokoski did not make me feel good or bad. It was done because it was necessary. I knew that sooner or later I would have had to fight or kill him. He was like a mad dog.I bathed in the river. I had a few new bruises on my face and my ribs hurt a little but it was nothing that a little time wouldn't take care of.

After breakfast Lieutenant Miller gathered up all his men. He told them. "We have orders from General Crook telling us that we have got to make all the Indian tribes surrender and come into the Reservations. If they don't come in, our orders are to take the field and bring them in. Tom Davis, who I'm sure you all know, will train us on the best way to do this. He will be treated as Second in Command of this troop by all of you. If you want to live through this coming campaign, I suggest you listen to and follow his instructions."I told them. "First, I'm going to tell you what you can't afford to do! The first thing to remember is the Indians want to kill you. The only way to stop them is to punish them every time you fight them. I'm training you so that maybe the Indians will respect you and decide not to fight you. It could save many lives on both sides. The Comanche, Navajo and the Apaches are the best light Calvary in the world. You must not let them pick the place and time to fight or they will slaughter you. They don't want to just steal your horses or weapons. They want to kill you. Don't go out looking for them unless you have plenty of water, ammunition and food and men. They can live off the desert. They will know where to find water almost anywhere they are fighting. Don't ever show fear. They can smell it if you afraid. They won't fight unless they can kill you without losing many men. Trooper Wales made a lot of mistakes. He stayed too long in one place. Most of the time the Indians will know when you take the field against them. They will try to ambush you and kill you if you make any mistakes. You should be nervous when you see them but you must really watch yourselves when you don't see them. If things go really bad, save one bullet so they don't capture you alive."

Chapter Three

We began the next morning. Lieutenant Miller had the soldiers up at 4:30. I had told him I would stay one month to help train the soldiers because I felt sorry for the troopers. After looking them over I knew that a month of training would not be enough to save all of them. It might save some of them. At 5 A.M. orders were given that the Company would move out in twenty minutes. Every one should have enough water to last a full day. The August sun had not penetrated the chill of the night. The Company did not depart in twenty minutes. After waiting 20 minutes more than that I took them out.

I told the Lieutenant, "If the Indians had attacked you and it took you 30 minutes to get prepared, most of you would be dead! Make your men carry their rifles and rations with them all the time." They were a sorry looking group. I wanted to teach them a lesson. I rode about five miles into the desert. I didn't follow a straight line. After two hours in the saddle I stopped. I dismounted, telling the troopers, "You are now on foot in hostile territory. What do you do?" The sun had begun to take its toll on some of them. I picked the one I thought was in the best shape to send back with the horses. He had not shown any weakness. He had most of the water left in his two canteens. I sent him back with two men who looked as though they were about to have a heat stroke. They took all of our horses back with them.I told the remaining troopers, "Consider yourselves under an Indian attack. You have at least ten hours before help can arrive. What do you do? The first thing is to check your water and ammunition."Some of the troopers didn't have any water. They had already finished it. Others had a little bit left. A few had half a canteen remaining. I made them check their ammunition. Only a few of them had 25 bullets or more. I sensed the troopers were beginning to get upset with me. I didn't care. My job was to train them enough to save most of their lives. I told them;" If this were a real Indian attack you would be as good as dead. The ones not killed by sundown would wish they were dead. The sun can and will kill you. The Indians will surely kill you. Mistakes and carelessness will get you killed." The soldiers milled around and looked like they didn't believe me.Sergeant Butch Gaston gathered them around him after putting out the perimeter guards. He told them a story about his experience with the Apaches. Before he was transferred to the Tenth Calvary he was in the Fifth Calvary at Fort Apache. He had been with the Fifth Calvary for five years. He told them of a patrol that had run into trouble because a brand new Lieutenant wouldn't listen to some good advice. Sergeant Gaston had been leading the patrol since he was the top NCO. He was ordered back to the fort by the Lieutenant to try and save a man that was as good as dead. If he could have stayed with the patrol, the tragedy wouldn't have happened.The Calvary patrol was made up of twelve men, not counting Sergeant Gaston and Second Lieutenant Roger Berry, who had graduated from West Point, second in his class. He had studied the military tactics of all the major leaders from all over the world. Genghis Khan, Alexander The Great, Napoleon and Robert E. Lee had been part of his studies. He had not studied Geronimo, Cochise, or Victorio. He didn't know "The Apaches" were the best fighting men in the world. Sergeant Butch Gaston was sent with him because he knew when and how to fight the Indians. The Mission of the patrol was to map the water holes around Fort Apache. The patrol had been out one day. It was about 11 A.M. when they stopped to rest the horses. The hot weather had made them sweat most of the water out of their bodies. Sergeant Gaston suggested they take the blue coats off and use the top of their long handles for a shirt since they were cooler, being more or less white depending on how dirty they were. The Lieutenant said, "His patrol will wear their tunics. They would look like troopers and not tramps."Private Greenbaum found him a boulder to get behind to relieve him self. He didn't notice the hole under the rock. The soft warning rattle of the snake meant nothing to him. The giant rattlesnake had been in the hole since his hunting trip for prey early that morning. He had a deeper hole he generally used but the sun got hot too quickly for him to get back to it. The hole was just deep enough to keep the sun off him. Since snakes are cold bloodied, they have no way to heat or cool their body. The heat would have killed him. The stream of water landed right on the snake's head. He shook his rattles furiously. Private Greenbaum ignored it. The snake struck upward where the heat pits under his eyes sensed an enemy to be. His fangs hit Ed's boots about an inch from their top. Ed screamed and jerked his leg. The fangs penetrated his Calvary boots and lodged there. Ed jerked his leg repeatedly trying to shake the snake off and stop the liquid fire burning in his leg. Every time he jerked he got another shot of venom in his leg. Butch Gaston knocked the rattler off his leg. Private Jessie Tatum shot the snake before Sergeant Gaston could stop him. The Apaches probably already knew where they were. The shot made sure they knew. Butch cut an x over the two holes and sucked some of the blood and venom out. He knew he couldn't save Ed's life no matter what he did. Ed Greenbaum was a dead man after the first strike He knew it was useless. The giant snake had injected enough poison to kill Greenbaum and ten others on his first strike. Butch Gaston took Lt. Berry aside and told him; "There is absolutely nothing we can do to save Private Greenbaum. We need to be thinking about the others now. The Mission has been compromised. The Indians know where we are. I suggest we start back to the fort." Lieutenant Berry had been told in West Point that the officer in charge always made the decisions. Sergeant Butch Gaston was shocked when Lieutenant Berry said, "You are going to take Private Greenbaum back to Fort Apache while we continue our search for water holes." It was a death sentence for the detail. Lieutenant. Berry made it an order for Sergeant Gaston to take Greenbaum back to Fort Apache right away. Butch Gaston tried to tell how dangerous it was several more times before the Lieutenant threatened to tie him up and send him back with a guard. Sergeant Gaston had no choice. He started back with Private Greenbaum who was already unconscious. Two hours from the patrol Greenbaum quit breathing. Sergeant Gaston reported to Captain Andrews, made his report, then requested permission to go back after the patrol.The second man on the patrol who knew something about Apaches was Corporal Richard Martin. He had been point man in his outfit during the "War between the States." He also rode scout for a caravan going to California. His wife, young son and daughter were third in the fifteen-wagon caravan. They entered a pass that made Richard nervous. Richard looked the pass over very carefully. He felt uneasy so he rode up to the canyon's end. He saw no sign of any Indians so he turned to ride back. Geronimo signaled to his braves to open fire. The mules pulling the first and the fourth wagons were killed, blocking the pass. The rest of the caravan backed up and formed a defensive circle. The first four wagons were isolated. Richard hauled his horse around and rode as fast as he could back to his family and his wagon. He had told his wife to put the children behind the second seat if they had any trouble. She was to sit there and wait for him. She had his double barrel shot gun. Richard told her to shoot only one barrel at a time.Richard got almost back to his wagon when a shot from Geronimo knocked him out of his saddle. The Apaches were swarming over the two wagons in front of his wagon. Lone Wolf went into Richard's wagon. Richard heard the boom of the shotgun. Claire had shot both barrels blowing Lone Wolf and the front curtain out of the wagon. Jatos was right behind Lone Wolf with his war club. Richard got up and ran toward his wagon although he was badly wounded. He got there just as Jatos came out of the front of his wagon. Richard shot him in the face. He jumped up on his wagon and looked into it. His family was dead. He spun around to check on the other two wagons in front of him. Apaches swarmed all over them. As he started to climb down, an arrow hit him in his chest punching through him. It knocked him out of the wagon and he landed on his back hitting his head on a rock. In less than five minutes the Apaches killed every one but Richard in the first four wagons. Richard was just hanging on. He looked dead. The Apaches thought he was dead. They cleaned out the wagons and disappeared into the rocks. They lost two men, the ones killed by Richard and his wife. It took the men in the wagons behind them a long time to come and check on the first four wagons. They were afraid the Apaches were waiting for them. Bill Seagraves, the Wagon Master, finally came by himself to check the wagons. The Apaches were gone. Richard was the only one alive in the first four wagons. He was just barely alive. They put young boys driving the four wagons. They used all their spare mules and two horses to pull them. Richard was put in the bed of Pete and Josie Polton's wagon. The Wagon Master cut the arrow's point off and pulled the arrow from his chest. They soaked the arm and chest and back wounds in alcohol and then cauterized them with the heated blade of a knife. Richard bounced along in the wagon for six days with a fever of 102 before he came to. He knew he was going to die if he didn't get out and walk. His hatred for the Apaches kept him alive. He walked only a few hundred yards at first, gradually building up to over a mile. He never talked about his family or the mass grave they were buried in. They reached Fort Apache in four weeks. He sold his wagon, his furniture and his horses and joined the 5th Calvary with the rank of Corporal. He had only one condition. He wanted to kill Apaches. He figured his time was coming. He tried drinking to forget his family. He couldn't get drunk. It just made him mean. He had lost his stripes twice. He had been at Fort Apache for two years. He was on the patrol with Sergeant Butch Gaston. Butch took him aside and told him, "You will have to keep the Lieutenant straight. Don't let him fall for any of the Apache tricks."They had been out two days and had not found any water or any Apaches. Victorio knew exactly where they were. He wasn't ready for an all out war with the white eyes. He hoped they would turn around and go back to Fort Apache. Lieutenant Berry made his second mistake. The old maps showing the water holes were not accurate. They never had been. He turned straight for Victorio's stronghold. Chato, who had been watching them, rode back to tell Victorio they were coming. Victorio still tried to avoid them by sending out four of his Apaches to fool the troopers. They would lead the troopers away from his camp. Richard Martin spotted them and told the Lieutenant they were decoys. They kept going right toward Victorio's village. The clash had been inevitable. The blue coats had to run into Apaches sooner or later. Victorio sent out his braves in force. He thought the blue coats would run. He didn't know West Point graduate Richard Martin was his opponent.Lieutenant Berry took the high ground, dug in and waited for the Apaches. There was no shade. The hot sun took its toll. Lieutenant Berry saw about thirty Apaches on their horses just out of rifle range. He had been taught that if all other things fail, you charge.Corporal Martin had waited two years for this. He led the charge. Sergeant Gaston would have taken them in the opposite direction. The bugler blew his horn to tell the Apaches the troopers were coming. They just opened up and let them through. They killed three of the blue coats as they swept past. In the hand-to-hand fighting that followed, Corporal Martin got his revenge and died happy. Lieutenant Berry upheld the honor of West Point by charging and dying bravely. The Apaches were happy because the white eyes were so dumb.

The twelve troopers killed five Apaches. Cpl Martin killed two of them. The troopers were lucky they were all killed quickly. The fight

Victorio didn't want had started. Big Man, who was six foot six got a new name. He was now called White Killer. He had killed three of the soldiers himself. Corporal Martin was one of them. Since the blue coats had died honorably the bodies were not mutilated or their scalps taken.Victorio moved his village closer to the mountains. It had started. The Apaches would never again stay in one place for a long time. The soldiers always returned in force. Sergeant Butch Gaston told them how he had got to the site of the battle with twenty- five troopers. They were a half day late. Victorio had moved his village. Sergeant Gaston could read the signs and he knew exactly what had happened.

He told the disgruntled men. "If you want to be dead heroes, like Lt. Berry, don't listen to Tom Davis. If you want to survive and go back home one day to your families, do what he tells you to."I made them get rid of all the surplus equipment. I told each man, "Pick up a small pebble and put it under your tongue." Find a good place with some shade. Make the Indians come to you. Make every shot count." I continued. "Conserve your water. Take small sips. Kill the leaders of the Indians if you can. Sometimes they will quit and go home if they think their medicine is bad. Die bravely if you have to die. Make them think all troopers are brave men who don't fear death or they will think all soldiers are cowards. This has been a hard day on you. You will have harder days. Let's go back to the base."I took my two extra canteens that were still full and passed them around to the ones who had no water, saying to them. "Only a small sip, we have a long way to go!"It was a battered, thirsty, tired troop of men that came marching back to their camp. Their water was gone and they were carrying four of their fellow soldiers when they got in but they came in feeling better about themselves.Sgt. Gaston and Tom reported to Lieutenant Miller while the men drank all the water they could hold. It made them sick just like I told them it would.Lieutenant Miller asked, "How did they do?"Sergeant. Gaston said. "We would have all been killed if it had been real!"I surprised him by saying, "They did all right. All they need is training and to get into better shape. We have a month to do that."Jedrokoski was taken from the hospital and sent back to Fort Prescott. He got better but never recovered fully. The Army discharged him as unsuitable for duty. He made up his mind that he would see Tom again one day and he would. He didn't want it to be too soon.Every day I made the soldiers run. I also trained them in what to expect from the Indians. Lieutenant Lin Miller joined them, doing the same training his men did. At night Tom, Butch Gaston and Lieutenant Miller went over the day's training. Lieutenant Miller told Tom how he had come home from the war. He was a Captain in the Fourth Illinois Regiment.

He had found out that his wife had not been too lonesome while he was gone. They tried to put it behind them but it didn't work out. He gave her and her boy friend his blessing and joined the U S Army. He had been sent West as a First Lieutenant. He was a good man and a good Officer even though he had been turned down twice in his promotion to Captain. Promotions were slow during times of peace. The Defense Department still didn't call this a war. The men respected him and listened to him.

The men gradually improved. They listened to me and did what I said. I reminded them constantly of the lack of water. I told them. "Before you go on a trip into the desert, drink as much water as you can hold. Take two full canteens with you. Remember to make as little noise as you can. Keep scouts a good distance in front of you. The scouts may be able to fire their rifles to warn you. You may have less than a minute to get ready. One mistake can get you killed. The Indians can smell your soap and your body odor even in the darkest night. "Four men had fought Indians before, Lieutenant Miller, Sergeant Gaston, John Logan and Ira Goodnight. Ira was the half-breed son of Charles Goodnight, the man who made the cattle drive to the miners in Montana. They said it couldn't be done. Charles sold his cattle for twenty five to fifty dollars a head. He got rich. He sent Ira to the University of Chicago to find himself. He didn't. Charles Goodnight told Ira. "No one cares whose son you are or if you are part Indian or not. They will judge you by your actions and if you keep your word." Ira majored in women and gambling. He flunked out and joined the Army. His enlistment was almost over.Four weeks after their first trip into the desert I took them back out. They were soldiers now. Each man had two canteens full of water. They wore white or brown shirts. Each man had fifty rounds of ammunition. Each man had stripped down to the bare essentials. I knew they would have to learn some things about survival the hard way but now at least they had a chance to learn. I told them. "Always expect an ambush. It could happen to you any time." I continued; "See that Barrel Cactus. Its juice is bitter but it will keep you alive." He cut a hole in it and gave some of the pulp to Private Wages who promptly spit it out." I put a wad in his mouth and chewed all the liquid out of it. All of the troopers tasted it and to a man didn't like it. "One day it will taste like honey to you." They had a good day and I was pleased with them.They rode out again at the break of dawn the next day. They had about two hours before the sun hit them full force.

I got that feeling again. I had pointed out to the troopers earlier that four Indians had crossed the trail four hours before we got there. Some of the troopers probably didn't believe I could know this. We rode on. The chill on the back of my neck got stronger. The insects were not chirping. I knew it couldn't be a large war party or they would have attacked us already. I gave the troopers a break from riding. I told the Lieutenant, "I'm going to slip back and around to the right, someone is over there." Lt. Miller kept the men talking, all the time wondering what was over there. I slipped off my horse and silently made my way to the back of the knoll I was concerned about. Two Navajo were slightly below me. They were watching the soldiers who were several hundred yards away. They never heard me as I came up behind them. Each of them had his rifle trained on the soldiers. They were laughing at the soldiers and having a good time. They were making fun of the soldiers. I knew Victorio would have shot them for being so careless.I hit Manito with the butt of my pistol and pointed the pistol at Kasko. When Manito came to his senses he saw me sitting there with my pistol aiming at him and Kasko. It took him a minute to remember where he was. I prodded Manito and Kasko making them walk back to the soldiers. I had an idea! I asked the Lieutenant, "Who are the two best shots in your company? It turned out to be James Slidell from Tennessee and Joel Forbes from Illinois. I explained to them what he was going to do. Both men grinned.We put blindfolds on the Navajo. We tied Manito to a Cottonwood tree. We put some tin mess kits on each side of Manito and one between his legs. At my signal Slidell began to shoot the mess kits. Forbes continued as Slidell ran out of bullets. I shot last. The repeating rifles sounded like a Gatling Gun. Manito knew he was as good as dead. We shot the mess kits to pieces. Bits of metal from the mess kits cut into Manito's legs and torso. None of them were very serious.I cut Manito and Kasko free and told them. "You are free to go. Tell your chief that the white eyes have guns that never miss and that Lone Eagle of the Apaches and his medicine is now with the white eyes." They ran away stumbling and falling as they ran. Manito's eyes were black and bleak. How could they fight against guns that shot forever and didn't miss? They would tell the chief of the guns that never ran out of bullets and now "Lone Eagle-The White Apache was now with the white eyes." .He showed the troopers how to find where water could be. Insects, especially bees, will lead you to water. The difference in the green coloration of plants might show that water was under them. Barrel Cactus has enough liquid in its pulp to help you survive even if you don't like the taste. The men had learned some lessons on survival and I was ready to begin my journey home. This time they stayed out all day and walked their horses more than they rode them. They understood that their horse was more valuable than they were. They stood a chance now. They rode proudly back to their camp. They took pride in being a part of the Tenth Calvary.That evening I went into town. I stopped at Reed's Mercantile Store to buy supplies for my journey home. I had $128 in my pocket. It was the money the Lieutenant had paid me. He paid me an extra month's pay. This included the money for the horses of the dead Navajo. I bought a can of peaches. I got the clerk, the one with my list of supplies, to open them for me. I speared a peach half with my knife. I walked out on the porch and finished eating the peaches. While drinking the juice I noticed the saloon across the street. I was curious since it had music coming from it I walked over to it. It was called "The Wild Horse Saloon." It was where Jedrokoski and his cronies went to when they came to town.The swinging doors opened into a room of semi-darkness. The light from the door and the two dirty front windows was the only light available. Oil lanterns lined the walls but they were not lit. The odor of smoke, sweat and lantern oil filled the room. It was stifling. I started to turn around and go back outside. As I turned I noticed a table where a poker game was going on. One man in particular was looking at me. I stopped and looked back at him. I could tell he was an evil man.A player piano sat against the back wall. It had about three songs that it played over and over again. It played all the time. One of the songs was (Clementine.) No one but me was interested in it. It played about half of it before it started over again. I would have liked to have gone over and looked at it but I sensed something about to happen. The man in black never took his eyes off me.

Chapter Four

The man wearing black sat facing me. I could tell he was the most dangerous man in the place even though he was not the fastest gun. I saw him lean over, and whisper to the man sitting next to him on his left. The man looked me over.This was the man Ron Jedrokoski had worked with in town, the one who had bought all the stolen merchandise that Ron accumulated. I had messed up a good thing for him. He didn't make a lot of money from Ron. It was the principal of the thing. Ron's cronies were eager to tell us all the bad stuff about Ron and the saloon, after his terrible beating. Ron had been taken to Fort Prescott. Black Jack was mentioned by all of Ron's cronies. I walked to the end of the bar. I didn't want anyone behind me. I put my package down on the bar and casually kept my rifle aimed in the general direction of the man in black.The man spoken to got up, and left the saloon. He went out the back door. The door squeaked as he opened it and again as he shut it. It would warn me if the man tried to slip back in. The bartender made it his business to light the oil lamps and then go to the other end of the bar. The man in black whispered to the man on his right. The man walked up and leaned on the bar. He was about ten feet from me. While his face, and hands, and clothes were filthy, his guns were spotlessly clean. The guns were worn way down on his hips, tied down. They were right where the gunman's fingertips came to. The little light given off by the oil lamps bounced off the clean guns. Another man got up and walked over to the wall, away from the man in black. They had boxed me in. Since I had not taken my finger off the trigger of my rifle, I was ready for them. I would kill the man at the bar first. He would be the fastest. The man in black would be next. The gunman standing against the far wall would be last. He would be the slowest.If you asked me how I knew this, I couldn't tell you. I just used my instincts.One of them might get a bullet into me. It wouldn't stop me from killing all three of them. I watched the eyes of the gunman at the bar. They were as black as the darkest night. He would start the action.The gunman licked his lips and started to turn toward me when Lieutenant Miller came through the swinging doors of the saloon. The gunman at the bar looked over to the man in black for his instructions.The man in black shook his head. The gunman at the bar put his hands back up on the bar. He looked at me, grinned and slowly shook his head. The gunman standing against the wall turned away from me. Lieutenant Miller asked me, "Are you ready to go back to the camp?" I nodded my head, never taking my eyes off the man in black. It had been close. The Lieutenant had stopped a killing. I knew for certain I would have killed the man in black. I figured he was doing this because of Ron. Lieutenant Miller didn't realize that he had kept it from happening.He went out the swinging doors. I followed him out. The small man that had left by the back door was standing on the sidewalk to our left, leaning on a post. The man pulled his gun. He was going to shoot one of us in the back. I reached behind my neck and pulled the short throwing knife I kept there.In one quick motion I flipped it at the gunman. It stuck in his throat. He dropped his gun, tried to pull the knife out. He kind of went up on his tiptoes, staggered backwards, gurgling as he died. He fell half way into the alley beside the saloon. Blood ran from his throat. I stepped over to him, pulled the knife out, and wiped it clean on the man's shirt. I put it back in the scabbard I wear behind my neck. I told the Lieutenant; "The man in black set this up. The two gunmen inside were going to try to take me. They got the message to call it off from the man in black when you walked in. The gunman outside didn't get the message."

"Why did they want to kill you?" The Lieutenant asked? I shrugged his shoulders. "Probably because of Jedrokoski."Before Lieutenant Miller went inside to see the man in black, he told me, "The man is Black Jack Ketchum. I've had trouble with him before. He killed a man two nights ago. I understand the man he killed had just won some big money from him. Black Jack accused him of double-dealing. No one would testify differently so I had to let him go. "The Lieutenant went back inside and got Black Jack. He brought him back out side with him. The Lieutenant asked him, "Is this your man?" He pointed at the dead man."What if he is? I can't keep up with everybody that works for me. This has nothing to do with me."I told the Lieutenant how they had boxed me in. The Lieutenant asked me, "What would you have done, if I had not walked in?"

"I would have killed all three of them, I would have made sure I killed this man." I nodded my head at Black Jack.Black Jack paled a little. He hadn't considered getting killed. He believed me because of the way I said it.He looked at me differently now. He hadn't believed half of what he had heard about me. He didn't like me. He didn't believe in many things, especially stories of heroic people. He thought that almost everyone would commit any kind of evil deed to get something for himselves.He would be more careful next time. He thought that killing me might loosen the town up a little for the action he had planned for later on that night. Lieutenant Miller told Black Jack, "I ought to hang you for this. I would if I had any proof. If you are here tomorrow morning when the sun comes up, I will hang you."Black Jack shrugged his shoulders and went back inside to play cards.They walked back to their horses on the other side of the street. A drunken cowboy bumped into me. The cowboy staggered and almost fell down. He told me, "Nobody gets in the way of a Texan. Draw your gun."I slapped the Texan upside his head with the barrel of my pistol. The Texan fell next to the horse-watering trough. I didn't hit him hard enough to really hurt him. I just helped him pass out from the whiskey he had consumed. The Lieutenant shook his head, looked at me and said, "What is it with you? Do you wave a red flag in front of everyone?"I laughed and said, "It does seem like folks out here want to test me." The Lieutenant and I rode back to the Army camp. I wanted to be on my way back to the ranch of my father the next morning.

It was not to be. A rider from town galloped up to the sentry before daybreak. He wanted to see the Lieutenant. I heard the man coming. I was already up and dressed when the man got there. I was waiting for the camp to come to life. The man told Lieutenant Miller," Black Jack has robbed the hotel and saloon and killed two people doing it."The Lieutenant looked around and saw me standing nearby. "Tom, the man who tried to kill you has robbed the hotel and saloon. He has killed two men. He and his men have been gone about an hour. Would you help us track them down?" It didn't take me long to make up my mind. Black Jack was a man that needed killing. It took the Lieutenant thirty minutes to get ready to ride. He had eight troopers with him. I thought, "The Apaches would have been after Black Jack in less than a minute. No wonder the white eyes always lose a battle."Black Jack had ten men with him, according to the man who saw them ride out of town. I knew that some of them must have kept out of sight since most of them had not been in the saloon. We rode through town. We met the cowboy from Texas. He was sober now. "Black Jack got my money, when he robbed the hotel. Can I go along with you?"The Lieutenant nodded, even though the cowboy looked at me when he said this. With out taking his eyes off me the cowboy asked me. "Are you the one who cold cocked me?" I nodded my head. The cowboy said, "Good, I'm glad that you did. Alcohol and me don't mix. I would have gotten killed, or hung for killing someone, if you had not knocked me out."The trail was easy to follow. The trail split about four miles out of town. By now it was light enough to see clearly. Half the outlaws had gone toward Medicine Canyon. The other half had taken the trail to Chimney Wells. They were the only water holes for miles around.Lieutenant Miller told me. "Take three troopers, the cowboy, and take the trail to Chimney Wells. I will take my five troopers and follow the ones going toward Medicine Canyon."I wondered why the outlaws had made no effort to cover their tracks. They must have known someone would come after them. I saw an empty whiskey bottle beside the trail. Then we found another one and another one. The men had also stolen bottles of whiskey along with the money. I knew why they had not been concerned. They were drunk. I knew the hot sun and whiskey would not take long. We found another empty bottle. I could tell by the tracks we were trailing five men. I had the cowboy, the half- breed, Ira Goodnight, and two soldiers with me. I noticed that both Ira and Cowboy could read the trail fairly well. I could tell by their actions. The two other troopers were just along for the ride. Both of them were tenderfeet.We approached Chimney Wells. I made a motion telling them to stop. I gave my reins to Ira when I dismounted. I went toward the water hole on foot. I could hear drunken laughter coming from the wells. I got close enough to see that all of the outlaws were drunk, except one.The drunks did not pay any attention to the man who was sober. He kept telling them, "We had better move on. We are making too much noise. The Navajo and anyone else pursuing us can hear us a long way out."I knew I could have taken them by myself if I had needed to. I decided to see how the troopers, and cowboy handled themselves. Cowboy was assigned one side. Ira was put on the other side. I took the rear. The two troopers came in from the front. I yelled out to the outlaws, "Throw down your guns and stand up with your hands up."One of the drunks pulled his pistol and shot it. It didn't come close to any of us. It got the outlaws killed. I shot one of them. Ira got one and cowboy got one. The troopers kept firing even after the outlaws were down. I stopped them from shooting.The sober man was the only one alive. He had been shot through his chest. He was propped up against a rock. He still had his pistol in his hand. I yelled at him to toss it away from him. He did. I walked up to him.The outlaw told me, "I knew this was a dumb play. I knew Black Jack was no good and he would get us all killed. I figured that I would have to kill him myself one day. Now look at me. I'm not going to get the chance."As he spoke, pink froth came out of his mouth. He was hard hit. I knew he wouldn't live long.The outlaw spoke again. "Maybe you can do me a favor? Maybe you will run into that sidewinder, Black Jack, again. If you do, will you kill him for me? Tell him that Ted Wilkie asked you to do it."I told him I would. The cowboy started going through the pockets of the dead men. He found a little money on each one of them. The wounded outlaw fumbled in his pocket and gave a pouch with silver in it to me.The troopers rounded up the spare horses. They stripped the dead outlaws of their guns and ammo. They didn't want the Navajo to get them. They carried the dead men a short distance away from the springs. We didn't want to contaminate the water hole.I looked at the dying outlaw and asked him, "Where has Black Jack gone?" The outlaw coughed up a little blood .He was drowning in the blood that was filling up his lungs. He told me, "He mentioned Abilene, and Chicago a few times. I hope you catch up with the skunk."I asked him, "Do you want me to leave you your gun with one bullet in it. The Navajo will be coming. They will have heard the shots. I wouldn't wait too long if I were you."The outlaw nodded his head. He might not need the bullet. He could feel his life slipping away from him, but then again he might live longer than he thought he would. He didn't want the Navajo testing him.I lay the pistol down beside the outlaw. I led the men out the side of the waterhole and rode parallel to the trail we rode coming in. I kept several hundred yards from it.I thought, "The cowboy and half-breed handled themselves well. "I suddenly felt a chill on my neck. I held up my hand. I motioned for them to go down into a small ravine. Ira led my horse down with the others. I concealed myself and watched the trail we had come in on.A war party of 20 or more Navajo rode over the rise. They were following the tracks the outlaws and the posse had made. The Navajo didn't ride as well as the Apaches or the Comanche, but they were formidable enough. They sat their horses well. The Navajo moved swiftly down the trail. The last one sensed something. Maybe he smelled a little dust in the air. He turned and started back toward me.I got my bow ready. The brave was only twenty feet from me when a shot sounded. He wheeled his horse around and rode after the others.I turned the outlaw horses loose. I made them run away from us. I figured the Navajo would rather have five good horses than lose men in a firefight with us. They would figure that we had repeating rifles.I led them cross-country until we cut the tracks of the Lieutenant and his men. We met them another mile down the trail.Lieutenant Miller had found the same thing. The outlaws he caught had whiskey with them also. All of them had been killed. Black Jack was not one of them.I thought, "Black Jack doesn't face much danger himself but he sure does get a lot of his men killed."The cowboy got all his money back. Eighty-seven dollars was a lot of money to him. Black Jack had escaped with over $5000. Everyone who had lost money got a little back.It was the most money the cowboy ever had at one time.I rode point as we rode back to town. I didn't really believe that twenty Navajo would attack eleven men with repeating rifles. I was right.When we got back to town, the cowboy asked me, "What do you plan to do now?" I answered, "I haven't thought much about it, I have to go back and find out about my folks." Cowboy told me, "I've got an idea. Can you meet me in the saloon this afternoon about five o'clock?" I nodded.Ira Goodnight overheard us. Ira looked at me and asked if he could come too. The cowboy looked him over and agreed to Ira coming. I nodded my head again.We met as planned. The wife of the dead saloon owner opened the bar as usual. Life had to go on. She already had men standing in line waiting to ask her to marry them. She knew that she was a good catch. She was not a beautiful woman, but she was attractive. The fact that she owned the bar made her most attractive. She would not be single long. A good single woman attracted all kinds of men in the West.I met with Ira and the cowboy. The man I nicknamed "Cowboy" was Kelly Sunday. He was born in the panhandle of Texas. His father had lived there all of his life. He had a scrub ranch that existed only because many Texas longhorns ran wild in the brush. Cowboy had enlisted in the war on his sixteenth birthday. He wasn't patriotic. He didn't care about slavery. They didn't own any. He just wanted to get away from the ranch. He joined in 1864,and fought in three major battles. He had been at Appomattox when Lee surrendered. He got back home three weeks after some Comanche had burned the cabin he and his father had built. His mother and father had been killed. He was the only child they had. He stayed long enough to sell the land to their neighbor. It was sold at a bargain price. The neighbor gave Cowboy forty-six dollars for it.

Chapter Five

After finding his parents killed by Comanche, Cowboy took the money and rode south to Nuevo Laredo, Mexico. He never looked back. He got in a poker game in Nuevo Laredo and won 30 more dollars. Rosita, the bar maid came with the money. She led him to her house and Cowboy stayed with her for two days. He was in love for the first time in his life.Rosita didn't tell him that she was the Sheriff's girl friend, or that the Sheriff was out of town. The Sheriff returned. Cowboy went back to the saloon for another bottle of whiskey. He had left most of his money at Rosita's house. He went back to her casa and met the Sheriff there.Cowboy had never backed away from trouble in his life. If the Sheriff had not slapped Rosita, Cowboy might have left peacefully. He told the Sheriff that he was staying as long as he wanted to. The Sheriff drew on Cowboy, who was slow. The Sheriff was slower. Cowboy shot the Sheriff in the right shoulder. Then for good measure he shot him in the left shoulder. He got his money and left town one jump ahead of a posse. He hadn't had time to go back and see Rosita since then. He was going back one day. He figured she had been worth the trouble.He rode to Austin, Texas and joined a cattle drive that Jesse Chisholm had organized. Cowboy's problem was that he spent money faster than he made it. He also thought of himself as a fast gun. He had lived up to now, only because he had not met a fast gun. He had killed a couple of men who thought they were. If things didn't change, Cowboy would meet a real fast gun sooner or later.Cowboy told Ira and me his idea. He wanted us to become partners and go on a cattle drive with Jesse Chisholm. He thought we could pool our money and buy a few cows. They could take them with them on the drive. Cowboy thought Chisholm, who was really a good man, would let them do it.Cowboy told us. "In Texas, steers are worth three to four dollars. In Abilene, Kansas they are always worth fifteen dollars or more a head. They ship them East on the trains."Ira had also been on the cattle drive with his father up into Montana. Some starving gold miners paid anything Charles Goodnight asked for them. He got up to fifty dollars a head for them.The timing was good. Cowboy had nothing to go home to. I had been gone a long time. A few more months wouldn't matter. Ira had one more day left on his enlistment. He was all for being partners with Cowboy and me.Ira fancied himself a good poker player. He had earned all his spending money at the University of Chicago by playing poker with the well to do students. He had made a little money playing with the troopers. He had to be careful with it because of Jedrokoski. He was down on his luck now and had only seventeen dollars. He would get twenty more dollars when he got his discharge.I was the one with the most money. I had $128. Cowboy had eighty- five dollars. With the 250 dollars we might buy up to seventy- five or eighty longhorns. It would be a start. If they sold for fifteen dollars each, we would have over 1000 dollars between us. It was a lot of money to us, more money than Cowboy ever dreamed about. Ira was not all that impressed with the amount. His father had plenty of it. I didn't think about it at all. Money was not that important to me. I only wanted enough to get by on. I thought about what the dying outlaw had said. "Black Jack had mentioned Abilene, Kansas." I wanted to keep my promise to the dying outlaw.Cowboy thought we should go to Abilene and look up

Jesse Chisholm, who lived there when he was not driving cattle. We could ask him if we could go with him on his next drive.I had been gone from the ranch over ten years. A little more time would not make any difference. Besides, I might make a little money that might help my family out. I agreed. Ira was doing what his father told him to do. He was trying to find out who he was. He did not like being a half-breed. He would not go back home until he made something of himself. He wanted to go with us, if we would wait one more day for him to be discharged.Cowboy had one burning desire. He wanted to be rich and go back to Nuevo Laredo, and get Rosita. He just might kill the Sheriff too.All of us felt good about the partnership. The next morning Lieutenant Miller told me, "I'm sorry you are leaving. We sure could use you bringing in the Navajo. I do understand though. I hope you find your family alive and well. "He discharged Ira twelve hours early so we could leave. I wished the Tenth Calvary well.

It is time for me to follow my own path that Ussen has for me.We rode out of Tucson. We were going to Abilene, Kansas. It was over 600 miles away. We bought more supplies for the trip. I became the leader. It just happened. I always rode point and always made the decisions on the trails we would take.Ira joked about us being partners.

"Who would ever believe that a white Apache, a half-breed Cherokee, and a dumb Texan could get along as partners."All of us were strong in our own way. Cowboy was twenty-eight. I was nineteen. Ira was twenty-four years old. Neither Cowboy nor Ira ever questioned why I, the youngest, became their leader.As we traveled the trail, our personalities became more apparent.Cowboy talked all the time, enlarging on the truth. He made quick judgments. He got angry quick, and got over it quick. He did not worry about anything. He was game enough to try anything. Cowboy thought that he was faster drawing his gun than Ira and me. He had killed two men. If he had known how many men I had killed, he would have had nightmares.Ira was a lot more serious. He had to stop and think things out before he did it. He didn't talk much and was kind of moody. He didn't get mad often but he never forgot it. He might or might not forgive it.I thought that Ira was the way he was because he was a half-breed. Ira had fought a few fistfights and a couple of knife fights. He didn't want to but he had to kill one of the men he had to fight. Ira didn't talk as much as Cowboy did. I didn't talk as much as Ira did. I didn't need to. When I said something, I meant it. I was good-natured. I didn't look for faults in the others, if it didn't put us in danger.I learned quickly how Cowboy would react in any given situation. It took me four days to figure Ira out. Ira was caught between the white and the Indian world. I was too.I had felt a little like Ira did when I became the son of Victorio. I did most of the hunting since I used a bow. I did most of the scouting. I picked where we would camp. Ira and Cowboy took turns cooking and building fires. Most of the time we did not use a campfire. When I sensed danger we ate what we had cooked the night before, or did without. I always scouted for miles around them before I would allow a fire to be built. On a few occasions we went a couple of days without food. That is, Ira and Cowboy did. They would not eat the grubs, bugs and raw snake that I ate. They tried some of the food and gagged. Going hungry bothered Cowboy a lot more than it did Ira. It brought back memories of the times of near starvation back at his father's cabin. Back then it had been feast or famine. The longhorns provided enough food or they went hungry.Each of us gradually accepted each other the way we were.Cowboy would say to Ira, "Sometimes I don't believe the White Apache is human. He doesn't seem to get tired. He doesn't get hungry, and I've never caught him asleep."Ira responded. "He has to make up for the way you are. "He laughed when he said it. Cowboy laughed too. They could cut close to the truth and joke about it now.I could sense when trouble was ahead of us. One day I knew that something was going on in front of us. I motioned for Cowboy to be quiet and I got off my horse and slowly walked up the small hill. I crawled the last few feet. A large gang was riding toward us. They were almost a mile away. I could feel the meanness in them. I went back and got Cowboy and Ira. We circled far to the right of the men. We watched the men ride right over our tracks without seeing them. I told them, "They may be bad, but they are not smart. A small party of Apaches would cut them to pieces."

None of these men were true Westerners.A few days later, I felt the chill on the back of my neck again. We were in northern Texas. I pulled up and got us off to one side, behind some trees. It was fortunate that enough grass was there. It stopped our horses from kicking up dust. Over thirty Comanche rode by us in single file. I could hear Ira catch his breath. They were all tall, slim men who rode their horses like they were part of them. Each of them had war paint on. Several of them had tufts of hair hanging on their lances. Fresh scalps had been taken.They were two hundred yards away from us. I waited for them to ride out of sight. I wondered why they had not sensed us. I would have. I waited a few more minutes and then we rode a lot faster than we had been riding. I didn't want the Comanche to cut our trail and follow us. If they did I wanted some distance between us.Smoke on the horizon told us where the Comanche had come from.Five miles away we found the remains of a family of five. I looked at the slaughter and wondered why anyone would expose his family to this. The burning cabin had not been completed long. A well had been dug. The father had been tied to the side of the cabin and shot with arrows. He had been shot in places that would not kill him quickly. Then they set fire to the cabin.His wife and 10-year old daughter had been murdered in front of him. A fourteen-year old boy and his younger brother had evidently put up a good defense. They hadn't scalped or mutilated them. They honored their bravery by leaving them whole.I walked over to the well and looked down into it. The sun was almost straight overhead. The well was about 18 feet deep. It only had a couple of feet of water in it. A part of the carcass of a horse was floating in it. The Comanche had eaten the rest of the horse.Cowboy wanted to go back and find the Comanche and kill all of them.Ira was mad, but he wanted to think about it before they went back. I shut off all discussion. I told them, "We cannot help the dead by getting ourselves killed. Some things are meant to be. The settlers, who settled here in the middle of Comanche land, have paid a terrible price for their mistake. It is time for us to move on."Cowboy wanted to bury them. I told him, "It matters not what happens to the body. The spirit is no longer there. We do not need to bury anyone out here. The animals of the land will take care of it."They mounted up and rode out. He finally got on his horse and followed us. He had tears in his eyes.Each of us now accepted the quirks in each other's personalities. After I had scouted around to make sure no one was close to us, we sometimes played poker. Ira brought several old decks of cards with him. I had never played poker before.It didn't take me long to catch on. Cowboy believed in pure luck. He didn't play the odds. He would draw for the middle card in a straight or three cards to make a flush.Ira was the opposite. He didn't bet until he had something, then he bet heavily. Cowboy suggested they play for money. He lost all of his money within two hours.Ira lasted two hours longer. I saw Ira cheat several times during the game. I called him on it on the last hand.I told them. "Cowboy, you don't play cards well at all. You need to find another way to lose your money. Ira, you don't cheat well at all. It will get you killed one day. We will never play for money again."I got up, leaving the money in front of them. I walked out into the darkness.Cowboy put his hand on his gun. "How long have you been cheating?""From the first day I started playing," Ira responded, smiling as he put his hand on his knife.They looked hard at each other several minutes before Cowboy chuckled, and said, "The White Apache is right, you don't cheat well and I don't play cards well. Both of us had better leave the card playing to the Apache."The card game was never spoken of again. I gave them back their money.Cowboy practiced drawing and pointing his gun. He wanted to get faster. He showed Ira and me how to do it. The holster was tied low down on the hip. The gun was just in the holster. At a count of three, Cowboy would draw and aim. He didn't shoot because I wouldn't let him. It made too much noise.Ira and I practiced the fast draw. It gave us something to do to break the monotony. It didn't take long for Cowboy to see that I was getting faster and faster. Ira told him, "The White Apache is faster than you and me put together." It gnawed on Cowboy. He had to find out. I made my circle around the camp and found everything all right. Cowboy asked me if it was ok to shoot our pistols.I thought about it a moment before saying that it was.Cowboy got some of the cards from an old deck of Ira's. He put a card for each of us on a tree. He, Ira, and I drew at the count of three.I shot three times before Cowboy got off one. Ira didn't even shoot.Cowboy told me. "It isn't just speed, you have to hit what you're shooting at." We walked over to where the cards lay on he ground. Both of us had knocked our cards off the tree. Cowboy's shot had nicked the edge of the card. Mine had three holes in the center of my card.Cowboy couldn't believe I was that fast and that accurate. He had to see me do it again.This time he heard the three shots before his gun cleared his holster. Cowboy had once thought that he was the fastest gun around. It shook him up to see that I was so much faster than he was.It might have saved his life that I had beat him so easily. Cowboy never felt that he was real fast again.I told Ira and Cowboy, "Don't aim the gun, point it like you point your finger." They tried it and both of them broke into a smile when they hit their cards almost in the center.Ira thought he was good with a knife until he and I started playing around with them. I did like the Apaches do when they teach knife fighting. I cut two sticks from a limb. I made them about the length of our knives.Ira was glad they were sticks instead of knives. He would have been butchered. He never even came close to cutting or stabbing me. I could cut him anytime I wanted to.I showed them how to shoot my bow. I told them, "Think the arrow into your target, and it will go there." Victorio had said the same words to me. Cowboy never did master the bow. Ira was adequate with it. I thought it strange that Ira, who was half Cherokee, had never shot a bow before.I also showed them how to fight barehanded, Indian style. Both Ira and Cowboy had bruises to show for their gameness. I told them, "I hope your life does not depend on your skill with the bow or hand to hand fighting." Both Cowboy and Ira were amazed at the ease I did things. They were almost in awe of me. I discouraged this because I wanted them to be independent. Without knowing it, both of them picked up some of my mannerisms. I smiled when I noticed this.All of us practiced the quick draw every day. Ira got so he could hit the card most of the time. Cowboy hit it in the center most of the time. I could shoot three bullets to their one bullet. I also could shoot two arrows to their one bullet.Ira told Cowboy, "If he fights against the Indians, I'm going to help him. If he fights with the Indians, I'm still going to be on his side."Cowboy was second best with the rifle and pistol. Both of them acknowledged that I was the best with all the weapons. Ira was second best with the knife and bow. Ira told them how to play the odds when playing cards. He told them how to bet heavy when you're lucky and when to cut back or drop out when you are not lucky. He could never beat me. I had that sixth sense when I needed it. I could even tell what Ira and Cowboy were thinking. I quit playing with them after several weeks on the trail. It was my sixth sense. I bet my good hands and dropped out on my bad ones except when I was bluffing. I liked to bluff a lot. I generally got away with it. Before I quit playing them, it got to be an obsession with them to beat me. Cowboy continued to play just like his personality. He took chances, and tried to draw impossible hands. He rarely ever got them. Ira lay back until he got his cards, then he bet all he had. I dropped out on my bad hands and on Ira's good hands. I caught Ira once with a good hand. I had a better one. Ira raised as many rocks as he had. Rocks were all I would play for. Ira had a full house, aces and tens. I had four sixes. Ira jumped up and almost stepped in the fire when he saw my hand. They gave up trying to beat me.

We entered Kansas.

Abilene had been made by the railroad coming through it. It was like all western towns. It was two towns made in one. One part of town was for the respectable people and the other part was for the people like the cattle herders who came to town to spend money or to find a job.Cattle had been shipped from Abilene to Chicago and New York for some time now. When the big cattle herds hit Abilene the men had to let off steam and catch up on all the things they had been missing during the long months on the trail.Abilene offered something for everyone, and a few things that nobody wanted. Zachery Scott had built the stockyards on land he owned next to the railroad. In one year he became a rich man.Cowboy liked Abilene, even though he had only been there once. He knew that Jesse Chisholm stayed at the Stockman's Hotel when he was in town.Tom, Ira, and Cowboy were amazed at the size of the town. It had over 2000 permanent residents. The people, who didn't stay long in any town numbered more than that.

Chapter Six

We had stopped for the night. I told them to watch out for themselves and moved quickly out of the light of the campfire. Cowboy and Ira took the strap off their holsters so their pistols would be loose. Both of them looked away from the campfire. They knew bright lights affected their vision for a while. They had their rifles lying next to them.Someone hollered, “We’re coming in to the campfire.”Cowboy shifted his weight a little so that he faced the place the voice came from.”Come on in. Keep your hands where we can see them.”Ira heard a noise from the other side as well. Both he and Cowboy stood up. Four men approached the campfire from different directions. The man who had yelled out to us spoke again. “We saw your fire and wondered if we might get some coffee.”Cowboy noticed the grin on the man’s face and the way he looked around the camp. The man spoke again, “You boys by yourselves?” It sounded like he was telling them something rather than asking them. Ira replied. “Yeah, Cowboy and I are looking for work. Times have been pretty tough on us.” The four men had gotten close enough now for the light from the fire to make them visible enough to be seen easily. The men gave the appearance of wolves about to pull down a sick longhorn.

They were cautious but sure of themselves. Each of them kept his hands close to his guns.Cowboy wondered how they had missed me as they came in. The man doing the talking winked at the other man across the campfire from him and said. "I hate to tell you boys this, but you are in for a rougher time."As he said this his hand flashed down for his gun. I was expecting this and shot him.My bullet caught him in his right arm. He was out of the fight before the grin left his face. The other three men were a trifle slower since they had waited for their headman to make his play. Cowboy shot the man closest to him in his shoulder. The man had stepped to the side and had his gun coming up when the pain in his shoulder from Cowboy's bullet turned him sideways. He dropped his gun.Ira shot his man in his knee. Cowboy started to shoot his man again as the man tried to turn back toward him. It wasn't necessary. I kept my gun on the fourth. His jaw dropped and he couldn't get his hands up quick enough. The action lasted only two seconds. Three out of four were wounded. The fourth man was in shock. I came back to the campfire. "There was only the four of them. They thought they had some easy pickings." The four men had only a few dollars between them. I took their guns and ammunition. After debating a few minutes about it, turned their horses loose after taking the saddles and bridles off them. We didn't want to be caught with horses that had someone else's brand on them. .I decided to give them a break. I took their guns a mile down the trail. At least they would have a fighting chance to survive.Their horses were probably stolen. We didn't want to explain how we got them if we met any friends or enemies of the four men.Two extra pistols were put in our saddlebags. They had two rifles also. I busted one, an old Sharps against a rock. The Sharps jammed too often. It would get you killed.I was pleased with the way Ira and Cowboy had handled themselves. I was fairly sure that the men had been by themselves but we packed up and moved a couple of miles away just to be safe. This time we didn't make a campfire.Cowboy asked me, "How did you know they were out there?"

"I heard them coming. I knew by the way they were coming, they were up to no good." Cowboy and Ira shook their head and looked at each other. Neither of them had heard anything. I told them, "You have to learn to listen."So far the trip had been a good one. We were just outside Salinas, Kansas. We had gotten to know each other pretty well now. We had dodged several bands of men by circling. One of them had been Kiowa and the others had been raiders.I felt the chill again. Someone was watching us. We were riding across a large meadow lined by trees.I said softly to Ira, "We have men on both sides of us. Be ready for anything. Tell Cowboy." They funneled us into a camp where over a hundred men gathered. One man detached himself from a big campfire and walked slowly toward us. "Get down and have a cup of coffee with us." He was friendly enough but I could tell that he was the headman and he wasn't giving us an option. Most of the men closed in around us. It was a tense moment. We dismounted and walked over to the campfire with the bearded man.A coffee pot sat next to the fire. It was close enough to keep the coffee hot, far enough to be able to pick up the pot. Several tin cups lay on the ground near the coffee pot. I picked up a cup, poured a little coffee in it, swirled it around, and threw it out. I had cleaned the cup a little. I did this with my left hand. I poured myself a full cup, set it down on the ground, and handed the hot coffee pot to Cowboy with my left hand. I kept my cup in my left hand while I drank the coffee. It was terrible. The bearded man noticed how careful we were. Ira and Cowboy were ready for action. Cowboy did exactly like I had done. He kept his cup in his left hand. Ira did the same. The bearded man smiled at the way we were careful and kept our right hands free. He nodded his head in approval.None of this was wasted on the men around them. The bearded man had been around careful men all his life. The men around us had their hands resting near their guns. They were careful men also.I blew on the rim of the tin cup, and took a swallow of the hot coffee. I noticed the circle of men drawing in a little closer. The bearded man was totally at ease. "Where are you fellows heading?"

"Abilene, Kansas I answered. We're hoping to join up with a cattle drive."

"That's hard work. I could use some more fighting men. I pay better too, "the bearded man said.The men around them tensed up, waiting for our answer.I looked around, noticed the tenseness and said, "I guess we will move on, and try our luck in Abilene."The bearded man shook his head a little and the men around them visibly relaxed. I took one last swallow of coffee, not noticing how hot it was. I threw the rest on the campfire. Cowboy and Ira did the same.I straightened up and said, "We appreciate the offer, and the coffee. We may see you again one day."The man led us back to our horses. He spoke to me in a low voice that only I could hear. "What if I had insisted that you join us, or die? How many of us would you three get?" I looked into the man's eyes and said, "I guess maybe eight or ten of you, but you would have been the first." I laughed as I said this.The bearded man laughed too. "I thought so. If you change your mind and want to make money a lot easier than herding longhorns, come on back."He told one of the men, "Take them through our lines. They're all right."Ira told me, "That's supposed to be what's left of Quantrill's Raiders. I heard two of the men talking about it."I asked Ira and Cowboy," Do you know who the bearded man is?" I hadn't asked his name and the bearded man didn't give it. I did know that the man was a good leader and that he was not a coward. Cowboy told them, "It sure wasn't William Quantrill. He died in a union prison after being wounded in a battle with Union troops in May of 1865."All of us thought that it was just a gang of outlaws, who had banded together and started using the old name of Quantrill's Raiders. Maybe a few of the men had actually been with Quantrill. Most of them were just fellows looking for an easy life. A lot of men who had ridden into that camp had not ridden out again.We could smell Abilene a long time before we got to it since the wind was blowing toward us. The stockyards were a couple of miles southwest of the town. Penned up cattle and their manure give off quite an odor.Abilene had been made by the railroad coming through it. The clothes were a little dusty but we could change them. The town covered almost a quarter of a mile. It was like all western towns. It was two towns made into one. Part of town was for the respectable people and the other part was for the people passing through and the ones who took advantage of the people passing through.

Cattle had been shipped from Abilene to Chicago and New York for some time. The men had to let off steam after three or four months on the trail. They had to catch up on some things they had been missing on the trail. Abilene offered something for every one and a few things no body wanted. Zachery Scott had built the stockyards on land he owned by the railroad. In one year he was a rich man. Cowboy had only been in Abilene one time but he liked it. He knew Chisholm stayed at the Stockman's hotel when he was in town. The town covered a quarter of a mile. It was a big town. Cowboy picked a hotel called the Plaza. It was on the wrong side of the tracks but it was a lot cheaper than the Stockman. We went to a Barber Shop, and got a haircut and a bath for 50 cents. We put on our dusty but cleaner clothes than the ones we had been wearing on the long trip.We rode over to the Stockman's Hotel. We walked in and asked the clerk if Jesse Chisholm was in. The clerk looked at us with distaste. He almost wrinkled his nose as he told us, "Mr. Chisholm is not in." They could tell that the clerk was thinking, "If he were in, he wouldn't see you."He was wrong. Jesse Chisholm was a man by western standards. He was a rich man but he did his own work. He had trailed herds from Texas to Abilene three times. He had fought Indians, outlaws, tornadoes, droughts, floods and snakes.He had been wounded twice. He had killed both of the men who wounded him, or rather he killed one of them and his men killed the other one. They hung the wounded bushwhacker along with three other cattle rustlers they caught. Jesse had left two of his own men on foot without food, horses or anything he had provided them. He caught them stealing extra rations and water during one of the dry spells on one of his cattle drives. He knew that a man who would steal water during a dry spell would betray you if he got the chance.He didn't care how much money a man had. If he had no honor, he wasn't worth shooting.He ate the same grub, and drank the same muddy water that his men did when he was on the trail with them. He was known as a totally fair, honest man. The Stockman was an ornate hotel. It had a dress and jewelry shop in it. It also had a barbershop. Room service provided food, a hair cut, or female companionship for the night, week, month or year. Chandeliers lit the place up. It had its own restaurant. Most of the people entering or leaving carefully walked around the three dusty cowboys as they left the hotel.Ira came up with a good idea. Mr. Chisholm liked to play poker. They might be able to find him in one of the saloons. We started with the one across the street. It was called "The Left Bank." The owner had spent a month in Paris, France and came home and changed his saloon from "The Good Luck Saloon" to its present name. Chishohm wasn't there so we moved on. Ira talked me into playing poker in the saloons as we searched for him. I started playing in the "Crazy Horse Saloon." The saloons on the other side of the tracks had smaller pots. I found out quickly they didn't play any better than Ira or Cowboy. In one saloon I beat a brawny cowboy to the last open chair. He started to say something but changed his mind when he saw me look up at him. I played a couple of hours and won about two hundred dollars. Ira and Cowboy watched my back. It was necessary in most of the saloons on the wrong side of the tracks. I won 425 dollars at "The Gold Mine Saloon." We worked our way back toward "The Stockman Hotel." The pots got bigger. "The Dead Man Saloon" was profitable for over a thousand dollars. We were back on the good side of town and for the first time hit some real gamblers. I won over 6,000 dollars. A couple of more saloons gave us their money. We had a crowd following us now. We hit Rudolph's about Eight o'clock. In the poker games I played in I had noticed little mannerisms that told me who had good cards or bad cards. One gambler rubbed his arm when he got good cards. Another gambler shook his cards a little when he wanted to bluff. One looked at the ceiling. I took all of their money. We had over twelve thousand dollars when we got to Rudolph's. The crowd following us was not allowed in Rudolph's. It catered to a better class of people.Cowboy, Ira and I were allowed in, only because I showed the doorman my bankroll. Even then the doorman hesitated.I saw a man dressed in black sitting at one of the tables. He had his back toward me but he still looked familiar.The table was in the middle of the room. I knew it had to be Black Jack Ketchem. I punched Cowboy on his arm to get his attention. I motioned to the table where Black Jack was sitting. I motioned for them to look around for anyone who could be connected to Black Jack.I stood there awhile and watched the men play. All of them were sure of themselves except one who was not very good at cards. He dropped out shortly after I arrived. Nobody made a move to sit down in the empty chair. Stakes were too high. You had to have 10,000 dollars just to get into the game. I walked over and asked, "Do you mind if I join the game?"The man on Black Jack's left motioned for me to sit down.Black Jack didn't blink an eye. "You have to show us ten thousand to play."The man on his left said, "Gentlemen, if we don't recognize the ones with enough money to play in our game, we shouldn't be playing poker."

Chapter Seven

I sat down. The man who had motioned me to sit down did the introductions. "I'm Jesse Chisholm. This is Jack Reynolds, he's in the mining business." Black Jack nodded his head.Jesse Chisholm continued, "This is Wyett Summers, he owns the bank. Next to him is Zachery Scott, who owns the stockyards." Jesse pointed to the last man, "That's Sid Morgan, he owns the Stockman's Hotel." I introduced myself. "I'm Tom Davis and I plan to go into the cattle business." When I said this, Jesse looked me over again. So did Black Jack. Jesse explained the rules to me. "It's Jacks or better to open. You can raise only three times to the card in stud and only three raises after the ante and three more after the draw in draw poker. We play pot limit. Dealer has the choice of the two games. Do you have any questions?"I pulled out my money, counted out ten thousand dollars. I got 10,000 dollars in chips from the man that Jesse had motioned over. I got a hard look from Black Jack.I put the rest back in my pocket. Jesse Chisholm told them, "Gentlemen, let's play poker."I played my game of cards. I watched all the expressions and movements of the men playing against me. I saw that Ira and Cowboy had taken places where they could see all around me. I wouldn't be

f I took Black Jack's money. Sid Morgan picked five-
ed at my hole card, a seven of hearts. I called a 500-
hery. I threw my cards in, when I caught a three of
aired his ace in the hole and won the pot. Black Jack
rs the banker played to the end and lost more on the
of us did. I got the deal and chose draw poker. I lost
e I folded. Jesse Chisholm won the pot with a ten
the third hand, drawing to a pair of aces and a ten.
von about 4000 dollars. Black Jack contributed
nt. Black Jack had built up a sizable stack of chips
e tried to buy a few pots before he found out that
vays stayed to see his hand. I caught a small
h, up to the seven. Black Jack happened to catch
a good hand also. Black Jack opened for a thousand. Jesse dropped out and the others played on since I did not bet too much. I only raised a thousand. I didn't take any cards. Black Jack called, took two cards. Black Jack got his full house. He had opened with three kings and caught a pair of fours on the draw. He just knew he had me beat. He smiled when he saw he had caught the pair of fours. Summers dropped out when Black Jack bet 2000 dollars. Scott called. Sid Morgan raised two more thousand. I raised it another two. It was a big pot. It had over thirty thousand in it. Black Jack spread his cards out. He smiled when Sid Morgan threw his cards on the table. He turned as pale as a ghost when I lay my straight flush face up. The momentum of the game changed. Black Jack started playing reckless. He won some big pots but lost more. The game went on for some time before Jesse, Black Jack, and I were the last three playing. Black Jack had won enough earlier to still have a lot of chips left. Jesse was about 30000 dollars ahead. I had also won about the same amount, maybe a little more. Black Jack had lost a lot since I joined the game. I had seen Black Jack dealing from the bottom of the deck a couple of times. He wasn't a lot better at it than Ira. The two times he cheated the pot had been large. I wanted to teach Black Jack a lesson. My chance came on

Black Jack's next deal. I had noticed that Black Jack seemed to win when he dealt the cards.Jesse had caught on to him also. He saw Black Jack deal from the bottom. On one of the earlier hands I had won, Jesse figured that Sid Morgan was bluffing even though he had dropped out early. When I raised Sid's bet Jesse smiled. He liked the way I played poker.Black Jack thought about it a long time before he folded. I called Sid's last bet instead of raising him. I didn't want to rub his nose in it. Sid had nothing but a king. I had a pair of sixes. Black Jack had folded with a pair of nines. He could have won the pot if he had stayed. It really made him mad. From then on he wanted to get even with me. Black Jack anted up 1,000 dollars. Jesse and I put in our 1,000. I caught three queens. I bet 3,000. Jesse bumped me 3,000 dollars. Black Jack raised another 3,000. I called. So did Jesse. The pot had $30,000 in it with just the opening cards. I took two and caught the fourth queen. I bet $10,000. Jesse had taken one card. It gave him a flush. He raised the bet $5,000. Black Jack took two cards. One of them was from the bottom of the deck. He raised Jesse 10,000 dollars. I called and raised him $7,000. It was all that I had left.Jesse looked at me and then at Black Jack. He had caught on that there was more than just a poker game going on between Black Jack and me. Jesse called putting $17,000 more in the pot. Black Jack would have like to have raised the bet again but couldn't since three raises was the limit. He called putting his $7,000 in the pot. Each man had $42,000 in the pot. Ira and Cowboy couldn't believe that anyone could play for that amount of money. I turned over my four queens. Jesse put his cards face down in the center. Black Jack started smiling at me. I reached over and pinned Black Jack's right hand to the table, just as he was about to turn his cards over. "All of your cards count except the one on the right. It's the ace of spades, you dealt it off the bottom." I said this in a quiet deadly voice. I told Jesse. "Turn over the last card on the right in his hand. It's the ace of spades"Jesse turned it over. It was the ace of spades. Jesse turned the other cards over one at a time. Black Jack had three more aces. Jesse turned to me, "Pick up the money, it's yours."I released Black Jack's hand. Black Jack went for his gun. Before it was half way out of his holster, Jesse and I had our guns out and pointed at him. Both of us had outdrawn him.Black Jack controlled his anger. It was not worth getting killed over.Cowboy and Ira kept an eye on the crowd. No one made any effort to help Black Jack. He must not have had his men with him in the saloon this time. Maybe they had smartened up. Black Jack was tough on men working for him. He had gotten a lot of them killed. Chisholm told Black Jack, "You're lucky this time. We normally shoot card sharks, especially the ones who aren't very good at cheating."The people around the table started saying, "Let's lynch him."Jesse stopped them from doing so. Only he could have stopped them from hanging Black Jack.I told him how Black Jack had killed two men in Tucson. Jesse told me, "We'll let the law hang him legally." He sent someone after the Sheriff.Black Jack turned and looked at me as the Sheriff led him away. "You haven't seen the last of me. I'll see you again one day. Then it will be my turn."Jesse took Black Jack's money still left on the table and gave it to me. It was over $2,000. I counted out $42,000 dollars, the amount Jesse had bet on the last hand and gave it to him. I counted out $5,000 each for Summers, Scott and Morgan. Jesse tried to give the money back to me. "Out here a man takes his own chances and pays for his own mistakes. You don't have to give us back any money."I told him, "I knew when I sat down, that he was a crook. I had the advantage over all of you." Summers, Scott and Morgan shook my hand and thanked me, just like Jesse had done. No one had ever seen anyone give poker money back before. I asked Jesse if Cowboy, Ira and I could talk with him a few minutes. I told him how we had come from Tucson to see if he was going to drive more cattle from Texas.Jesse smiled as he told them, "That's a coincidence, I plan to make one more drive. Why don't you men meet me in the restaurant of my hotel for breakfast? We'll talk about it then. Is 6:30 all right with you?"I was patted on the back as we made our way back to our hotel. The word got around quickly in Abilene. We counted the money I had won when we got back in our room. Even though I had given away $57,000, we had over $75,000 left. I was the only one who slept that night. We walked into the Stockman Hotel a few minutes before 6:30 the next morning. The same clerk was there. This time he was not so polite. "Mr. Chisholm has not mentioned you, and I'm sure he's not going to."About this time Jesse walked down the stairs and heard the conversation. He told the clerk. "These men are my partners, I suggest that you ask them to forgive you for your bad manners. I will tell Sid Morgan how you have treated the man who gave him back $5,000 last night."Even the clerk had heard the news about the poker game last night. The clerk turned deathly pale and apologized. He made sure we were treated first class, on the house. He couldn't do enough for us.As we ate breakfast, Chisholm's favorite meal, he told us of his plans to have one more cattle drive. "This will be my last one. The railroad has spanned the country and the need to drive cattle will soon be over."He never had a partner before, but he liked the way I had acted the night before. He took a man's friends as being like the man. He often told folks, "You can judge a man by the company he keeps."I told him, "Cowboy, Ira and I would like to buy some longhorns and drive them along with yours."Chisholm thought a couple of minutes on it and said. "I don't see any reason why we can't have two herds. I believe that the most we can trail at one time is around 5000 longhorns apiece. There are two trails. You can take one trail and I'll take the other."Ira and Cowboy knew from their past experience, that water determined the trail and the success of the drive. Chisholm would know where the water was since he had made the drives before.They talked most of the morning. The clerk checked regularly to see if they needed anything. Cowboy laughed. "It sure is nice to have money, and to have folks waiting on you." Chisholm smiled at the remark and said, "I wouldn't do much business with a man like him."Chisholm and the trio decided to meet in Austin, Texas in five weeks. Cowboy knew about Austin. Chisholm remembered him being on a drive with him. It helped him to make up his mind.Chisholm had an agent representing him in Austin. They would buy all the cattle they could from the small ranchers, who spent all year rounding up the wild longhorns. It was a lot quicker than having to round them up themselves after getting to Texas.Chisholm advised us to see Wyett Summers and put our money in his bank. He would give us a letter of credit. That would be safer than carrying all that money around. He told us to take a couple of thousand dollars with us.It didn't take long for Wyett Summers to see and accommodate us. I thought, "It's surprising how $5,000 makes us more acceptable." Being known now as friends and partners with Jesse Chisholm didn't hurt us either.Sid Morgan came into his hotel. He saw me, Cowboy, and Ira talking to Jesse. He came over and told us "A suite of rooms is yours anytime you are in Abilene. There will be no cost to you or your friends. Put anything you want on the tab. I'll take care of it."Both Jesse and Wyett Summers were good judges of character. They had to be. As we emerged from the bank, I happened to glance in the alley across the street. In it was one of the gunmen who had been at the bar in Tucson. He was drawing his gun.I pushed Cowboy into Ira with my left hand and drew my gun at the same time. Cowboy and Ira both fell down from the hard shove. My gun sounded three times. The gunman fired at the same time. His bullet slapped into the brick wall where Cowboy had been standing.The gunman looked down at his chest where three red spots appeared and seemed to be growing. He couldn't believe it. He took a step, trying to get his gun up for one last shot. It was too heavy. He fell forward into the street.The space between the trio and the gunman suddenly became clear. People moved away from them. They checked on the man. He was dead.I thought, " Black Jack has managed to get one more of his men killed." We sent a man to get the Sheriff. The Sheriff had been looking for us! He told us "Black Jack isn't in jail. He's gone. The dead gunman had busted him out earlier that morning. He had killed a deputy during the jailbreak."Later on a drunk in one of the cells was shown the dead gunman. He verified that he was the man who freed Black Jack. He was also the one who killed the deputy." The three of them spent most of the rest of the day looking for Black Jack. They didn't find him.I was ready to hit the trail. Cowboy and Ira wanted to spend some of their new riches. They wanted a night on the town. I wasn't interested in joining them. I didn't want to spend another night in town. I was tired of the odor and the people. I wanted some fresh clean air. I went south of town, several miles out, and camped. The wind wasn't blowing in that direction. The odor of the cattle didn't reach me. Ira and Cowboy were going to meet me the next morning. Ira and Cowboy agreed that they would not drink any whiskey after midnight. They would not drink again until the cattle drive was over.I told them. "It would be good if all my enemies were whiskey drinkers. It makes men do foolish things."At first Cowboy thought I was trying to tell them something. Then he realized that I was being honest with my feelings, just like he always was. I was not looking for a fight with them.They both knew I would not back from one either. Cowboy and Ira spent most of the night moving from saloon to saloon. They were both recognized as being partners with Tom, who was the hero of the town. Free drinks were given to them everywhere they went. The ladies of the evening made a big play for them, and their money. They were in the Crazy Horse Saloon when it happened.

Chapter Eight

Ira saw one of the ladies of the evening that he fancied. She was with a lanky cowboy who was growing angrier with Ira by the minute.Cowboy could see that Ira and whiskey didn't mix too well. Ira was about to go over and get the girl when Cowboy decided they had enough and had better leave before Ira got them in trouble.Cowboy was just sober enough to take Ira by the arm and lead him to another saloon. Ira began to cause trouble there too and in every saloon they hit. Cowboy hadn't believed me when I told him that Indians were not able to drink whiskey without going crazy. He believed it now. Ira began to get mad at Cowboy for interfering with his quarrels. Cowboy couldn't stand it any longer.He hit Ira in the jaw as hard as he could. Ira fell like a dead man. Cowboy got some help and put Ira across his saddle. He mounted his own horse, leading Ira's, and rode out to find me.They were two sorry looking cowboys when they found me. Ira was unconscious. Cowboy's eyes were red from having to stay awake. They found me about 3 a.m. where I said I would be.I put Ira on his bedroll. Cowboy was asleep in less than a minute. I woke them up at 5:30. Both of them were sick at their stomachs and had bad headaches. I threw water on them when they started fussing about getting up. It didn't improve their dispositions although neither of them wanted to tackle me about it.Both of them kept wishing they could die all that day. Neither could eat anything when we stopped late that afternoon.I didn't even talk to them. By the end of the second day they thought they might live. By then they even wanted to.Some nights we saw the glow of other campfires as we traveled toward Texas. We avoided them. I told them, "Only fools or large parties of men would have a big campfire on the prairie. We don't want to be with either of them."Once we came up on the tracks of unshod horses. They were going in the same direction we were.Cowboy was surprised when I continued following the tracks. Cowboy asked me, "How come we don't circle around them?" I told him. "If we circle around them now and they turn right or left they might cross our tracks, then we would have them following us. When we see which way they are going, we will choose the way we want to go. The tracks cut left after we followed them several miles. I watched that side carefully, looking for any sign that the Comanche had doubled back toward us. I didn't see any. I hunted with the bow when hunting was necessary. If a cook fire was lit it was a small one with wood too dry to smoke much. The fire was extinguished quickly. Most of the time the meat was half raw. I liked it that way. Cowboy and Ira didn't, but they ate it anyway.Cowboy and I each had a 50 caliber Sharps. It was called the buffalo gun. I shot purely by instinct. I allowed for distance and wind with out thinking about it. Cowboy tried to figure it out in his head. I had already shot before Cowboy could get set. I could hit my target regularly out to 700 yards. Cowboy could hit something big within 400 yards. Ira wasn't any good at all with the buffalo gun. He didn't own one, had never wanted one.We hit the Texas panhandle where all the longhorns were supposed to be. We stopped at every small ranch we came to. Someone had already been there.All the longhorns had been bought up. The ranchers had been paid $3.25 for each one of them. The men owning the small ranches had been glad to get that much.They found this was true all the way to Austin, the Texas town they were to meet Jesse Chisholm. They had bought 33 head of cattle. They met Chisholm in a cantina in Austin, Texas. He was sitting with a long lanky Texan.I didn't want to but I told Chisholm that we had found only 33 longhorns available on our way to Austin.Chisholm laughed and said, "Fellows, meet Jeff Cook. He's my foreman, and purchasing agent. I left some money with Jeff after our last drive to Abilene. He's been buying cattle for me since then."I was glad for Chisholm, but it looked like Cowboy, Ira and I were out of luck.Chisholm saw the way we looked. We had made a long trip for nothing. He grinned as he said. "Jeff has bought a few cows for you too."We waited to see how many cows Jeff had purchased for us.Chisholm went on, "The most cattle we can trail at one time is about 5000, that's how many I own. You fellows have 4400. That's all Jeff could find. I've paid Jeff for them. You can pay me for them when we settle up in Abilene. You owe me $3.25 a piece on them. You will owe Jeff twenty-five cents each on the ones you get to Abilene. How does that sound to you?" The three men whooped it up, or at least Cowboy and Ira did. They kept jumping around and hugging each other. Jesse laughed at them. Everyone was happy for them.I was doing some quick figuring. 4400 x 3.50 = 15,400.00 plus whatever it cost to drive them to Abilene. The trio couldn't believe it. Chisholm had taken care of them.Cowboy said it best. He blurted out to Jesse Chisholm, "It's no wonder you're rich. You're smarter than the rest of us." Chisholm laughed loudly when Ira and I agreed with Cowboy.Jesse told us, "Jeff will ramrod my herd. We will take the north trail to Abilene."He continued, "Quito will ramrod yours." He motioned for one of the several Indians standing nearby to come over.Jesse told Quito, "Meet the owners of the herd you'll ramrod to Abilene."Quito looked them over with his hard black eyes. He was a full-blooded Cheyenne.He and eight other Cheyenne had been on two cattle drives with Jesse. They liked and respected Jesse. On every occasion, Jesse had stood tall.He didn't like the trio. He made no effort to hide his feelings. He didn't think much of tenderfeet. He didn't like half-breeds, and he hated most Texans. They bragged and lied too much.He could sense that I didn't particularly like him either. Ira and Cowboy didn't like him at all.Quito did not like white men. He liked Texans and half-breeds even less. He and his Cheyenne had learned to exist with them, but that was all.Chisholm had found the Cheyenne to be his best men after he had proven himself to them. They had a fierce loyalty to a leader they respected. Every man on a cattle drive had to prove himself. They had to depend on each other.We would be tested early in the drive by the Cheyenne. Jeff Cook, who was hired by Chisholm to ramrod his herd, had bought the chuck wagon and supplies. He had his own crew. Quito was mad at Chisholm at first until Jesse explained that two herds would be driven to Abilene. "The trio needs the best ramrod; that's you. That's why you will ramrod their herd for them."Quito spoke some English. The rest of the Cheyenne spoke only a few words of it. They understood most of it. They acted like they didn't.Chisholm told Quito of the poker game. He told Quito how Tom had handled Black Jack. Quito was not too impressed even though he knew Jesse Chisholm was a good judge of character. He did feel better about the trio. Quito listened out of respect for Jesse, but he knew he would have to make up his own mind about me and the others.Chisholm was busy getting his herd ready to go. They had to do the same.The two herds were in separate valleys with only enough grass for three or four more days. Any more grazing would ruin it forever.Quito and Jeff Cook had already bought supplies, guns, ammo and two spare axles and axle grease for the chuck wagon before the trio got there. The most important thing on a cattle drive was food. They had to have plenty of that.The chuck wagon and the cook were not interfered with on a cattle drive. You didn't want to get on the bad side of the cook.The cook for this drive was a wizened old man, Bill Sager, who had seen many winters. He was a genius with a frying pan.Bill didn't have much of a sense of humor, unless it was he playing the joke on someone else. He was the only one that got away with practical jokes, since everybody liked to eat. He didn't particularly like the Cheyenne or anyone else. He got along with everybody.Each man had to have five extra horses in his own personal remuda.Trail drives were hard on men, harder on horses. Each man had to pick, and break the horses himself if they had not already been broken.Quito had rounded up the horses. He had broken only about half as many of the wild mustangs we needed. The other wild mustangs had been partially broken so that it wouldn't take too long for the ones who picked them to finish breaking them.When Ira, Cowboy and I showed up, we could tell a lot of the horses were still wild.One of them was a killer. The black stallion had tried to stomp Broken Bow after he had thrown him. They had saved the black for one of the three owners of the herd. They had named him Black Devil. It was the kind of joke they liked.Quito told each of the trio to pick and break one of the horses. He wanted to see if they knew a good horse, and if they could ride well enough to trail cattle.I picked the black stallion. Broken Bow smiled. The rest of the Cheyenne grinned.I rode my horse into the herd, worked the black stallion loose and lassoed him. The stallion fought me all the way. I got him to the corral where they broke the horses. No one offered to help me.I tied the rope holding the stallion to the pole in the center of the corral. I slid off my horse and grabbed the rope close to the pole. I kept talking gently to the horse all the while I worked my way up to him. I put a loop around the front feet of the stallion.The stallion was terrified. Only the whites of his eyes were showing. He had backed as far away as the rope allowed him to. He fell down several times. I pulled him up, speaking softly to him every time he fell. I worked up the rope, talking to the stallion all the time. No one could hear what I was saying to the horse.I picked up a rope halter. I got to the stallion. He tried to rear up. I held the rope firmly, not letting him do so. I put my hand on his neck. The stallion quivered, and tried to back away from me. He couldn't go any further. I rubbed his neck and back while I continued talking softly to him.It was obvious to the others that the horse had settled down. I slipped the halter over the horse's head. The stallion quivered all over. The rope bit was put into the horse's mouth.

The Cheyenne used metal bits. They gave more control, but they tore the mouth of the horses. I jerked the slipknot on the rope holding the front legs of the horse.I untied the rope holding the horse to the pole and vaulted up on his back. The stallion went crazy. He sun-fished, coming down hard on all four feet at the same time. He spun all the way around never slowing down. It jarred every bone in my body. I kept my mouth closed. I didn't want to bite off part of my tongue. The horse continued to buck, spin, and sunfish all over the corral. He tried to get me off his back by rubbing me against the fence. Several times he almost threw me.He began to settle down when he found he couldn't get me off his back.Cowboy opened the corral gate. The black stallion bucked right out the gate. I led him over to where the Cheyenne had gathered. The black stallion scattered them in all directions when he bucked right through them. Long Knife fell backwards and rolled under the corral fence to save himself. It got a big laugh from Ira and Cowboy.I let the stallion have his head. He took off as fast as he could run. I let him run it out. And he really could run. He was the fastest horse I ever saw. When the horse tired, I turned him and rode him back to the corral. I talked to him all the way.All of the Cheyenne, except Long Knife, nodded and smiled at me. At least I had proved I was a horseman. I took the stallion into the stable, took off my shirt, and wiped most of the sweat off him. I put my shirt on the horse's neck and talked to him.I fed and watered him before I left the stable. I left my shirt on the horse. I wanted the horse to feel comfortable and to be familiar with my smell.When the Cheyenne saw the scars that dotted my upper torso they decided that I was a fighter, since I obviously had been wounded and lived through the fights. That is, all of them except Long Knife, who considered himself a good rough and tumble fighter.Cowboy picked next and got the next best horse in the corral. Quito nodded his approval.Long Knife approached Cowboy and told him, "I had planned to take that horse. Pick you another one."Cowboy looked at Quito, whose black eyes were staring a hole through him. He knew he was being tested. He told Long Knife,

"You did not pick this horse when you had the chance. He is mine."Cowboy had his hand close to his gun. The gesture was not wasted on Long Knife. He started to say something, but turned away. The anger he felt showed on his face. Cowboy broke his horse in a short time.Ira picked a good mare and broke her easily. Quito told the trio. "Maybe you won't be totally useless on this drive. You three will ride drag when we start."Ira and Cowboy knew what riding drag meant. It meant dust up your nostrils, in your mouth, ears and all over your body.All of the Cheyenne smiled when they heard Quito tell them this. It was a smile that was friendly. The trio were beginning to earn their place. Drag was the place they put tenderfeet on their first drive until they earned the respect of the others.Both herds started about the same time. Quito pulled out first. We had been on the trail three days when Long Knife picked a fight with me. We had come only twenty-seven miles. We had made only six miles the first day.Chisholm's herd left a few hours behind us. You could see the dust from his herd by looking west the first and second day. Ira, Cowboy and I rode drag without complaining. We were covered with dust when we stopped for the night. I went up stream from the herd and took a bath. Ira and Cowboy washed off with water from the barrels on the chuck wagon.The fourth day the herd moved a little faster. A crusty old longhorn had stepped forward and took charge. He became the leader of the herd. We made 10 miles that day. Water determined how far the cattle could or would go in a day.The next day the longhorns kind of caught on and we made 11 miles. It was a good day for everyone except for Cowboy, Ira, and me.The dust had gotten worse. We were resting around the campfire eating the supper meal of beans, stew beef and bread when Long Knife picked his fight.Long Knife had been mad ever since Cowboy had taken the horse. He thought that I had deliberately tried to make the bucking horse run over him. He was right.It had been a long day. Every man on the drive also rotated as night guards. Ira and I were to be the guards that night.We had almost finished our supper. We were sitting on the ground a little way from the campfire.Long Knife walked by us. He kicked me on the foot as he went by. All the other Cheyenne were looking at me. They wanted to see how I was gong to handle Long Knife, who stopped and grinned at me. He was playing to the house now.I stood up slowly, and gave my tin plate to Ira to hold. I walked over to Long Knife, who had only wanted to ridicule me.I challenged him in sign language. "You are as clumsy as a woman in her last month before giving birth. Is it that you do not see well, or is it that you are too old for this kind of life?"All of the Cheyenne were surprised that I knew sign language. They were also surprised that I knew the insults also.Being called "like a squaw" was about as bad as it could get. They laughed at Long Knife. He was no longer their champion. Twice the joke had been turned on him.I issued him a challenge. I gave sign. "It is time to act as men, instead of children. We can fight with our knives or without them. I leave the choice up to you."Long Knife started to choose knives. He wasn't quite sure why he decided not to. He felt some hesitation in doing so. I was too confident. Besides I was a friend to Jesse Chisholm.We stripped down. Long Knife rubbed some smelly, greasy salve on his upper body. He offered it to me. I refused it.Long Knife was happy. At least he could hurt me and get even with me. He really thought he was the best rough and tumble fighter among the Cheyenne.Either fighter could stop the fight by giving up. Most of the time it was a fun fight between champions of different tribes. Occasionally it was used to settle arguments. Sometimes it ended with someone dying to settle the argument.

Chapter Nine

Long Knife grabbed at my arm. Then he rolled his body at my legs. He wanted to end it quickly. I moved out of his way, and kicked him in the stomach as he rolled by me.The Cheyenne laughed again. Long Knife jumped up. His temper got the best of him. He kicked out at my leg. It was a vicious kick. I waited to the last second before moving away from the kick. My foot shot out just as Long Knife's foot missed me. I knocked his leg out from under him. I already had two chances to really hurt Long Knife and I had passed them up. The Cheyenne knew by now that Long Knife was in for a real fight.Long Knife made another effort to grab my arm. I spun around him using my momentum to jerk him off balance.Before he could recover, he found himself flying through the air. I was on him before he could get up. I had him pinned on his stomach. I sat down on his back and locked one of his ankles with a hold that would break it if Long Knife continued fighting. White Killer had taught me the hold. Long Knife knew he could not beat me.He had two choices. He could give up, or he could suffer a broken ankle, or a broken back if I chose to go that way.He gave up. He looked at me and gave sign, "Where did you learn to fight?"I answered, "With Victorio and his Apaches."

"You are Lone Eagle, son of Victorio?" All of the Cheyenne began to murmur between themselves. All of them had heard of Lone Eagle. Long Knife turned almost as white as Cowboy. All of them gathered around me patting me on the arm as a sign of respect. Long Knife grinned at me, "I am glad I did not pick knives." From then on the trio was accepted on equal terms. I was accepted as one of their leaders, equal to Quito, who told them, "From now on, all the men will take their turns riding drag. Lone Eagle will ride in front for us. He will scout for us, and find us water." It made the trip easier for Ira and Cowboy. Sometimes they rode as flankers, sometimes drag, and every once in a while they were put in front of the herd. They did not do any scouting or riding as flankers for protection. Long Knife I were the only two who did that. We had to keep the old longhorn leading the cattle moving in the right direction.The heavens opened up and it rained on the seventh day out. The dust became mud. Dry washes filled with rushing water in just a few minutes. A few cows were swept away crossing a once mild stream.Some of the smaller stock got stuck in the mud. They were lassoed and pulled out. Luckily no lightning accompanied this rain.Quito and I made the decisions now. We decided to stop the herd for a day, since they had plenty of grass and water.The rain quit. We moved out on the next day. Three hours of hot sunshine dried out the trail some. In a short time it was hard to tell that it had rained at all.Several calves were dropped during the drive. The riders put them up on their horses and carried them back to the chuck wagon. The riders would put them on the tailgate of the chuck wagon until time to stop for the night.Most of the time the calves found their mother. Sometimes one of the other mothers would allow a motherless calf to suckle along with her own calf. It didn't happen very often. If the calf was refused, we had it for dinner. A lot of the time we had stew several days in a row since it was easy to make. The baby calves were not as tough as the longhorns.Bill Sager, the cook, didn't say much or waste much. He did make a good stew though. He made the best apple pie any of us had ever eaten. On a real good day we made eighteen miles. Some days we only made six or seven. We had to go as far as the water was each day or at least close enough to reach it the second day.The longhorns could miss one day but they made up for it when they stopped for water. They sure got ornery when they didn't have enough water.I stayed about five miles ahead of the herd finding water. Long Knife stayed a couple of miles closer to the herd. It gave us a better chance if we were ambushed. The longhorns could smell water miles out. They covered that last mile a lot faster than the other miles. We were in Comanche territory.Long Knife and I were out in front of the herd. We always rode point when there was a possibility of danger.Quito wasn't that much concerned about Long Knife or me. We could handle our selves. His responsibility was the longhorns. He let two of us ride point because one of us had to live through an ambush and get back to warn the rest of them. It was a good plan.We had two more hours before the herd caught up with us. Water was a mile away. It was only a small stream. It would be enough to slake the thirst of the cattle, and enough to give them some water to put in the barrels on the chuck wagon.I looked around and saw a Comanche sitting on his horse some distance from me. I had that cool feeling on my neck. I knew more had to be nearby. Three more rode out from the direction of the stream in front of me. I had no idea where Long Knife was. I had not seen him in over an hour.One of the Comanche rode forward while the others stayed about 100 yards from me. The Comanche held his palm out in the peace sign. He didn't look peaceful. He gave sign to me. "To pass through our land, you must give us some of the white eye buffalo."I noticed the war lance the Comanche held ready for action. I noticed the tufts of hair attached to the lance. The Comanche had taken new scalps."We come in peace. We will give you some of our cattle for food. We will give them to you as a friend. We will not give them to you to cross the land. It is not your land. It is Ussen's land."

"I am Broken Lance, War Chief of the Comanche. It is we, who decide who our friends are. You are not our friends."I looked hard at him. "We will camp here tonight. When we leave tomorrow, we will leave you ten steers as a token of our friendship. We would not like to make the women of your village sad because they lose their braves. If you choose not to be friends, you can start with me."Broken Lance walked his horse closer to me, so that he could get a better look at me. It shocked him that it was him that was being threatened instead of me, a white eye. His eyes glittered, "If you refuse to give us the white eye buffalo we will kill you and take all of them." We were only five yards apart. When he finished saying it, he drew back his arm to throw his lance. I drew my pistol so fast that Broken Lance didn't even see the gun come up. A surprised look came over his face when the bullet hit him in the chest. The second shot wiped the surprised look off his face. He toppled off his horse. The lance was still in his hand.When the shots sounded the other three Comanche came riding forward to attack me. I got my rifle out. I shot the last one in line fifty yards from me. I shot the second Comanche in line thirty-five yards from me. The arrow shot by the last Comanche might have gotten me if my black stallion had not sidestepped at the last moment. I shot the last Comanche as he was notching an arrow for another shot at me. He was only ten yards from me when he fell off his horse.I turned to look for the Comanche I had first seen on the rise to my left. I saw him racing away. I jerked my reins to get the black stallion after him. If he got away we would be knee deep in Comanche by nightfall.Long Knife popped up from behind a bush and shot the Comanche. He had been coming in the direction the Comanche was fleeing. He heard the shots. He would have been too late to help me with the four Comanche but he had planned to revenge me if I had been killed.Long Knife rounded up all the Comanche horses, except one that got away. It must have been a Comanche hunting party a long way from their camp, since we never saw any more Comanche.I rode several miles in the direction the Comanche had been fleeing. I saw no signs of any other Comanche. Long Knife rode back and told Quito.A week later I almost got killed. The herd had been bedded down for the night. They began to get skittish sometime after midnight. When the first ones raised their heads and began to bawl, the night herders should have caught on. The wind freshened and got cooler. The longhorns began to get up and stir around. The storm was on us before anything could be done. Lightning flashed and thunder rolled all around the longhorns.The longhorns were off and running in just seconds. They stampeded back toward Texas. Heavy rain started falling. I had changed horses earlier. Black Devil had been ridden several days in a row.It didn't take long for the Cheyenne and the trio to get after the cattle. The night herders spurred after them and were trying to turn them. If they could start the longhorns milling, it would stop the herd.I went over a small rise while riding beside the herd. I was almost to the front of it when my horse stepped into a hole and fell. I was catapulted into the air. I hit one of the few trees almost head on.They didn't find me until the next morning. Long Knife and Cowboy came back looking for me after they had turned the herd toward camp and had eaten breakfast. It took them all night to get most of the cattle back to camp. All of that day, and most of another day would be used to round up the stragglers.Two men had been missing. Gray Horse, one of the Cheyenne, and me. They found what was left of Gray Horse and his pony. He had been one of the night herders. His pony had gone down in front of the longhorns. There wasn't much left of him. I didn't come to until the end of the day. They were loading me in the chuck wagon when I opened my eyes. I managed to sit up before the headache floored me again. My vision was fuzzy.I tried again and was able to sit up. Quito gave me a concoction he had made from some herbs he had found. I drank the foul smelling stuff. I made a face but I did begin to feel better shortly after that. I lay back down and went to sleep. The next day my vision cleared. I had a headache for several days after that. I got up on Black Devil and resumed my job as point man. My headache ceased a few days later.That night the men entertained me by telling stories of people they had known that went crazy, blind or died from a lick on their head. All of them knew of people who had never recovered from being hit on the head. They seemed to enjoy telling me about it.Quito would laugh every time he mentioned that I must have a hard head. It wasn't that funny to me, although I accepted it. When we crossed into Kansas we met outlaws. I had that feeling again. I got up and left the campfire.I circled and came up behind some men that were approaching the camp. One of them hollered out, "Hello, the camp."Quito motioned for some of his men to get into the shadows."Are you friend or foe?"

"Friend," a voice answered from out of the darkness. I could see about ten horsemen, sitting, framed by the light of the campfire. I was close behind them. They were not aware that I was there."Come on in," Quito told the man. I saw the man dismount and walk into the circle of light given out by the campfire.The man looked around. They could tell that he was counting the men. He wasn't impressed by his count. Quito offered the man a cup of coffee. The man refused it.Quito asked him, "What can we do for you?""I have over a hundred men near us right now. We can stampede your cattle and kill most of you easily. We want a dollar a head or one third of your cattle."Quito acted like he was kind of dumb. "Let me think about it tonight? I'll let you know tomorrow morning which way we want to go."The man left smiling, thinking, "That was easy. We'll be a lot richer tomorrow."I didn't come back to the camp until hours later. I had trailed the men back to their camp. It was about five miles north of us in a grove of cottonwood trees. They have a few guards out. They are not very good at it.Quito had accepted me as the leader now. He waited for me to tell them what to do.

Chapter Ten

I told them where the outlaws were camped. I couldn't tell them how many of them were there since it had been dark. I knew that it was a lot less than the 100 men claimed by the outlaw. I looked at Quito, who nodded at me. There was no doubt about what we had to do. We would carry the fight to the outlaws. We got ready for war. The Cheyenne were looking forward to it. They had faced drought, floods, storms, and contrary longhorns. This was something they could strike back at. The Cheyenne put on their war paint. After thinking about it for a second, I did too. Ira, Sager, and Shasa, one of the Cheyenne, stayed with the herd. We left long before dawn. We were in position when the sun cast its first rays on the camp. Quito and I disposed of the three guards with our bows. Each man with us had a rifle and a pistol. Some had two. The Cheyenne also had their bows. All of them had been told to wait for me to shoot first. The man, the one who had talked to Quito about the money or the longhorns, was the first to get up. He stretched, scratched himself, and walked over to a tree to answer nature's call. He looked around, still half asleep. It took him a moment to realize that he didn't see any of his guards. He yelled for the men to get up. My arrow hit him in the chest. He flopped backwards. The other men, in various stages of undress, jumped up and tried to get to their guns. Some of them made it, most of them didn't.I gave them a chance to surrender. It would have been a turkey shoot. The outlaws were out in the open. Most of them had their boots off and were hopping up and down trying to put them on. They didn't have to worry about that long.The Cheyenne, Cowboy, and I were only 40 yards from them and we had them in a cross fire.Two men who got to their guns were shot. The others were quick to raise their hands. I stopped the shooting. Thirty-six outlaws were alive and unwounded. They knew a rope could be waiting for them when they surrendered.The outlaws numbered forty-two instead of a hundred. Six of them were dead. Santiago, one of the Cheyenne, was slightly wounded. He had chased a fleeing outlaw and had been shot in the arm.Quito was in favor of finishing off all the outlaws.Two of them looked too young to be involved in a gang of this type. "Whose gang is this?" I asked one of them. "It's Quantrill's," the young man said with pride.I recognized a couple of the dead men. "What happened to the bearded man who used to run it?"

"That was Major Murdock. J. W. killed him, shot him in the back." It turned out that J. W. was the one I had shot with my first arrow.I told Quito, "Take their horses and guns, leave them enough food for one day. We will let Ussen decide if they live or die."Quito looked at the outlaws and grinned. All of them shuddered. Quito thought it was a good joke on the men. He would have taken their boots also.The gang that called themselves, "Quantrill's Raiders," was destroyed. Major Murdock had kept them going. He had robbed only the towns that had lots of money. Only twelve of the men survived the trek back to civilization. The two young men didn't make it.It took us eight more days to get to Abilene. There were days that seemed to stretch on forever. The scarred old brindle steer kept the herd moving. They got in a day ahead of Chisholm.Cattle buyers approached them when they were still five miles from the stockyard. A cowboy had seen the herd in the distance and had rode in and told the cattle buyers.One of them offered eighteen dollars a head right then. He thought he might take advantage of us since we would not know what price the cattle were bringing.I had the idea that cattle must be bringing a real good price. The cattle buyer went to eighteen-fifty and then to nineteen. I told him we would talk after Chisholm reached Abilene.He was right. The stockyards were empty.Zachery Scott remembered Tom well. He told his man at the stockyard to take good care of Tom's cattle at no cost to him.They had started with over 4400. The tally at the stockyards when they finished counting was 4218. The calves, 14 of them, didn't count. They would help take care of any cows the buyer lost before he shipped them out.I made arrangements with Wyett Summers, the banker, to give Quito and his six Cheyenne enough money to last them until we sold the herd. Quito and the Cheyenne were allowed to stay in only two hotels in Abilene.They would be allowed in the Stockman only because Sid Morgan said they could. He owed that much to me. Quito didn't want to stay at the Stockman. He preferred a place on the other side of the tracks called the Outlaw's Nest. It was a good description.Indians were not accepted as part of the social life of Abilene. Most people thought all of them should be shot. They were acceptable only on the lowest part of the wrong side of the tracks.Sid Morgan kept his word. The three of us were given the best rooms in the Stockman on the house. All of us spent hours in the tubs filled with steaming hot water. We bought new clothes. I killed the rest of the night playing poker at Rudolph's. I found that I was something of a celebrity there. I didn't much like it. I did like the poker games and since money meant absolutely nothing to me, I couldn't lose. I won over $5,000.Cowboy and Ira were having a well-earned night on the town. They had kept their promise. They had not taken a drink all the time they were driving the cattle.They had a lot to make up for. It would cost one of them his life.They hit the Bar Z Saloon after midnight. I had already turned in. Both of them had drinks in most of the saloons they went into. They were minor celebrities who had too much to drink..Free drinks had been given to them almost everywhere they went.Cowboy thought how ironic it was that the second time in his life that he had money, he couldn't pay for a drink. They wouldn't let them.Cowboy had found himself some feminine companionship. She really smelled good. He had a nice glow on. The more he drank, the prettier she got. Ira had gotten drunk to the point that he forgot his Indian blood.He saw a girl that really attracted him. She was sitting on the lap of a cowboy. The cowboy was old enough to have gray sideburns coming out from under his Stetson. He had survived twenty-five long years as owner of a small ranch eighty miles from Abilene.He was just about as poor now as he was twenty-five years ago. Once a year he came to Abilene to sell a few cows, and let off a little steam. He had been married only two years before his wife left him for a drummer that was going back East. He didn't blame her.

No woman in her right mind would stay married to a cowboy with a small run down ranch. He was gone all the time trying to keep his cattle alive. He was not very tall either. He had fought a few times when people insisted on making fun of him by calling him "Shorty." He only let his friends call him "Shorty."The girl sitting on the cowboy's lap smiled at Ira. It was her job to smile at all the customers. It was enough for Ira. He was in love again.He motioned for her to come over. The cowboy had been looking over that way, and saw Ira's motion. He grinned at Ira and shook his head. He motioned that he had her now, for as long as his money lasted.Ira got up and walked over to the table the cowboy was sitting. The girl continued to smile at Ira. He reached out when he got there, and grabbed her hand. He started to pull her out of the cowboy's lap.The cowboy's voice was bigger than he was. It snapped Ira's hand and head back.Shorty got angry. He also was a little drunk. He normally would have sidestepped trouble if he could. This time he didn't care if he found trouble. It had been a bad day.

He said to Ira, "Go back to your wigwam, and leave the girls to us real men."It sobered Ira up some. He told the cowboy, "Shorty, you aren't big enough to back up that kind of talk." He straightened up and took two steps backward. The people around them in the saloon got real quiet, and moved away from them. The quietness spread all over the saloon.The old cowboy pushed the girl off his lap and stood up. He had to fight for everything he had ever gotten. He wouldn't back down now.They faced each other. Both of them had too much to drink. Ira waited for the cowboy to draw. The cowboy waited for Ira to draw. Someone dropped a glass on the floor. It started the action.They went for their guns at the same time.Ira did it just the way he had practiced. He was fast. Shorty, the cowboy, was just as fast. The shots from their guns sounded at the same time. Ira was a better shot. He hit the cowboy in the chest, just above the heart. It was where he was aiming.The cowboy's shot hit Ira in the head. He had been shooting for Ira's chest. Ira died instantly, six minutes before Shorty did.Ira had survived two cattle drives, two years in the Army, several fights with Indians, several fights with whites, only to be killed in a saloon brawl by an honest, drunken cowboy.Someone went and got Cowboy who was thinking about maybe settling down with Rosita. He sobered up quickly. He had known that once Ira saw a girl he liked he would not stop until he got her.It was too late for him to think about what he should have done. He should have stayed with Ira. He might have stopped the fight if he had been there.The girl told all of her future male companions how two men fought to the death for her. It seemed very romantic to her although she didn't waste a tear on either one of them.She soon moved on to her next man and then on to her next town.Cowboy had to wake me up and tell me how Ira had picked the fight and was killed because of it. Ira was buried in the town cemetery next to Shorty.I felt like I had lost a brother. However all of us knew that it could happen to us any time. It was a hard, uncertain life we led.

Chapter Eleven

Jesse Chisholm brought his herd in the next day. He had 4630 steers left. They had 8834 between them. They let the cattle buyers bid against each other for the cattle. They got $21 a head for them.Chisholm got $97,230 for his herd. Cowboy and I got $88,578.I gave Chisholm a check for $14,300. Jeff Cook got paid $1,051 for buying the cattle for them. Cowboy, Ira and I had made over $20,000 apiece in the two months it took us to drive the cattle to Abilene. They were rich men by any standard.Quito was given $600. It was a hundred dollars more than he expected. The other six Cheyenne were paid $400 each. He gave Quito the wages the two dead Cheyenne would have gotten. Since neither man had a family, Quito was told to divide the money, and the outlaw's horses between the ones left. They could also keep all the horses used in the drive. I had already given them the guns and money we had taken off the dead outlaws. Sager, the cook, got $500 and the chuck wagon. All the other expenses such as the beginning supplies came to $4200. We paid Chisholm all we owed him and tried to give him more. He would not accept it. He told them. "I don't make money off my friends." He grinned a little bit and added, "Except in poker."They had cleared $65,284 on the drive. Counting the $65000 they still had from the poker winnings, they had $130,284. Each of them got $43,421.I got Wyett Summers to send Ira's share to his father, Charles Goodnight.Cowboy had more money than he had ever dreamed of. I had never thought much about money. He still felt like the Apaches did. He had a good horse, food, clothing and weapons. It was all he needed.Thinking about Ira took away the satisfaction that both of them would have been feeling.They had a farewell dinner with Chisholm, Summers, Morgan, and Cooper. They were told to look them up if they ever got back to Abilene. Sid Morgan repeated his offer of free accommodations at his Stockman Hotel.I saw no reason to stay on in Abilene. Cowboy was ready to go back to his Rosita in Nuevo Laredo, Mexico.Quito, Long Knife, Broken Bow, and the rest of the Cheyenne also saw no reason to stay in Abilene. South of Austin looked good to them. They would be big men in their own rights when they returned home with all that money each of them had.Chisholm said that it was his last cattle drive. He was right. The Central and Union Railroads that had begun on each side of the country had met at Promontory Point, Utah. The country now had a transcontinental railroad.Cattle could be shipped from almost anywhere. The price of cattle would go way down. It would not be worth the trouble to have a cattle drive.Cowboy and I said good-by to all of our friends. Wyett Summers put their money in his bank and gave each of them a letter of credit that was good everywhere. Chisholm and his friends would have their card game later that evening. Nothing changed much in the west.Cowboy and the Cheyenne and I rode together as far as we could. When Cowboy and the Cheyenne turned south toward Nuevo Laredo and Rosita. I turned west on the old Santa Fe Trail. Quito and his Cheyenne went back to Austin. They touched their chest as a sign of respect for Cowboy and me. They rode away and never looked back. Cowboy almost went with me but he decided he had to see his Rosita.I struck out for Santa Fe and the ranch of my father.I told Cowboy. "If it doesn't work out in Nuevo Laredo, look me up around Santa Fe. We'll buy us a ranch together." We were like brothers now.Quito and his Cheyenne were like the Apaches and Tom with their feelings. When it was time to go, no emotion was shown or felt.

Chapter Twelve

I rode on to Santa Fe. I had no trouble on the way. It took me twelve days to get there. Although it was still hot, I could feel the change of weather in the air. Even the sun's rays felt different.I was riding Black Devil, who by now could anticipate what I wanted him to do. I could make him change directions, stop, run, or jump by the pressure of my knees. All Apache horses were taught that so the rider could use both hands on his bow and arrows.Santa Fe was hot and dusty. It hadn't rained for quite a while. I could feel the rain coming.I stopped at the first place I saw that I could get a meal. It was about four in the afternoon. I had not eaten all day, since I knew I would reach Santa Fe that evening.The cafe was in the same type building as the others on the street. It was a run down building made out of a little wood and a lot of adobe bricks.The wood had been bleached by years of sunshine and very little rain. It was almost shiny from the dust storms that scoured it occasionally.I walked into the cafe. It was big enough for ten or twelve people. It had a bar with four stools and two tables where four could eat. I had it all by myself.Bert Evans came out of the open door that led into the kitchen. He was of medium height, had a mustache that curled a little on the ends. His face was slightly pockmarked by a childhood bout with measles. I guess he was in his middle fifties. He might have been older. He had an apron tied around his waist.He had been part of the Santa Fe scene most of his life. He was where he wanted to be.He reached over, got the coffee pot off the little wood stove behind him and poured me a cup of coffee without saying a word.For a minute I wondered if the man could speak.Bert looked me over and said, "You're new in town. What can I get you?"From then on I didn't get to talk. Bert took my order of steak, potatoes, eggs, and biscuits. He asked questions, answered them, and made comments without waiting for me to respond to any of them. I had to remind him twice that I was hungry. When he brought the food he talked on and on.It was all right with me. I didn't want to talk anyway.The meal wasn't as good as Sager's, the chuck wagon cook, but it was better than my own cooking. I asked Bert. "Is there a place I could take a bath and spend the night?"

"There's a boarding house up the street run by a widow." When I left him he was still talking. That helped explain why he didn't have more customers.One other thing Bert said. "Look out for all the gunslingers coming into town." Bert watched me mount up and ride up the street. He thought, "I'll bet they don't bother that fellow none." I continued up the street. The old hotel was not in the best part of town, but it was on the right side of the tracks. It had seen better days.The board sidewalk ran the length of the buildings that made up this part of town. The old town Plaza was still some distance away, at the end of the street. Most of the buildings forming the Plaza were made of mud bricks covered with stucco.The boards of the sidewalk were uneven, and some of the sidewalk was covered with sand. The wind picked up the sand, played with it, and then dumped it wherever it wanted to.A wooden roof covered the sidewalk in front of the hotel. A wooden rail had been built on the right side, next to the sidewalk so people could tie their horses to it.A saloon, "The Palace," was across the street from the hotel. I saw one of the ill dressed, dirty men lounging on the sidewalk, look at him, and then go into the saloon. I didn't figure any of the men I saw were gunslingers.I walked up the three steps, and pushed the door to the hotel open. I looked back at the saloon. A red headed man had come to the door of the saloon to look at me. He nodded his head at me and turned away. The man, who had gone inside, came out flipping a coin up in the air.The red headed man was paying for information on the people who came into Santa Fe. A bell sounded when I opened the door to the hotel. I stepped inside.The old building had a smell to it that was different. It wasn't pleasant or unpleasant. It was the odor of age and wood oil. It smelled like it had been there a long time. I could also smell the aroma of coffee and the slight scent of a woman's perfume.A middle-aged woman, whose sad face made her look as though she had been having a bad time, appeared."What do you want?" She did not smile at me as she said this.I heard a door open and saw a girl, maybe eighteen years old, come through it. It evidently led to the kitchen. She had a fresh smudge of flour on her nose.I felt my heart beat faster. For a split second, I thought she looked like White Fawn. Looking again I saw that she did resemble her slightly.Suddenly, without knowing why, I became more nervous than anytime I had to face Comanche.The older lady smiled briefly when the girl came out. The lady looked years younger when she smiled. It was as if a weight had been lifted from her.She repeated, "What do you want?"

"I'm looking for a room and a bath."

"Are you sure you want to stay here? This is a respectable place. The other places are farther down the street."The young girl looked at her mother. She turned to me and smiled. "I'm Susan Estes and this is my mother. Her name is Mary. Pay no attention to her."She continued, "The room is a dollar a night, or five dollars a week. How long did you want to stay?"I surprised myself when I said, "I'll take it for a week." I gave her a five dollar gold piece.Mary said, "Meals are seventy five cents a day or $5 a week. Breakfast is from 6:30 to 7:30. Lunch is from 12 to 1:30. Dinner is from 5:30 to 6:30. If you're late you don't get any."I thought Mary might have softened up a little as she looked at me when she said it. I gave her another five dollar gold piece."Is there a place I can stable my horse?"

"Turn right at the corner of the alley. Zeke Calloway has a stable at the end of it."Mary had the last word. "We don't allow shooting, or carrying on in our rooms either." She did smile this time as she said it."Can I leave my saddlebags here while I go stable my horse?"I had $500 in gold coins in my saddlebags.Mary reached over and tried to pick the saddlebags up but couldn't. I reached down and picked it up with my right hand, and set them over against the wall.Susan looked at her mother when I left. "He seems like a nice young man."

"You can't tell anything about young men like him. At least he has some manners."I found the stable right where Mrs. Estes said it was.A small gnarled man, of undeterminable age, looked up when I rode into the stable."That's a nice horse you have there," he rumbled. He had a deep voice for such a little man. I had seen it several times before. Nature seemed to compensate when it shorts people on something else.Zeke smiled as he rubbed Black Devil on the neck. The deep lines in his face disappeared when he smiled."How much to keep him a week?"

"Two dollars if you want him watered and fed."Zeke continued to pat Black Devil on his neck. Black Devil liked it and didn't try to move away from Zeke. He was only the second man Black Devil had let rub him."That's good," I thought, "at least Zeke likes horses." I knew I wouldn't have to worry about my horse. Black Devil had never let anyone touch him but me."Be careful, there's some bad looking folks that stay in the saloon across the street from the hotel."It made me curious. It was the second time someone had told me about bad gunslingers.I decided to walk over to the saloon to see the bad men before I went back to the hotel for my bath.The same man went into the saloon to tell the red headed man that I was coming into the saloon.I got there while the red headed man was still talking to the man. I walked over to the end of the bar, and ordered a sasparilla.I noticed that everybody stopped and looked at me when I ordered it.A couple of the tables had poker games going. I watched the games a few minutes. I spotted the house gambler cheating right away. I didn't see anyone in the saloon that I would consider dangerous.One of the men playing at the table with the red head got up.The red head motioned for me to take the chair. I did.The men inside the saloon were wealthier than the loungers outside the saloon. None of them looked dangerous."Folks around here call me Red, I don't know why?" When he said this he laughed a little at his own joke."Are you new in town?"

"I'm just passing through."I took out $100 in gold coins and put them on the table in front of me. The gold caught Red's attention. We started playing.Red considered himself a good poker player. He told me how good he was.He didn't play like it. I caught on early that Red was a phony. I knew when Red had the good cards and when he didn't. The others at the table didn't play any better. I gradually won most of the money at the table. I was up $350 when the gambler from the table next to us asked if he could take one of the two empty chairs. I didn't even look up at him. "I don't play with tin horn gamblers who deal from the bottom."The gambler was directly across from me. I looked up at him as I said this."If you shake your arm to get to your derringer, I'm going to kill you."The gambler who had started to do just that, kind of blanched a little. Since I had my cards in my hands, the gambler thought that he could get his derringer out before I could get my gun out.The gambler debated about trying it for a few seconds before his nerve broke. He didn't want to bet his life on it."You have five minutes to get out of town, or I'm going to kill you." I said quietly.I won the pot. The gambler just stood there. He wanted to ask if he could go and pack his clothes.I looked up at him again. "You now have four and a half minutes to live."The gambler broke completely. He went outside and mounted his horse and rode out of town toward Albuquerque.One of the men followed him outside, and watched him go. He came back inside. "You scared the life out of him. He didn't even stop to get water."I looked up at the man who turned away after he thought, "I would have left also if it had been me."Red had watched the gambler leave with interest."Do you want a job?"I said, "No" and continued playing. I won $50 more before the game broke up.Red had got redder and redder as he lost. He was mad because he had lost most of the money I had won. "Just what do you do for a living?"I didn't even bother to answer him. I gathered up my winnings, got up and started to walk out.For one brief second Red considered shooting me in the back. I paused at the door. "I wouldn't even think about it, if I were you. Even if you are lucky enough to get a shot off, I would still kill you."Red turned redder when I said it.I knew Red was a four flusher. He wasn't big enough for the act he was putting on. He couldn't be the leader of whatever was going on. Some one had to be backing him. None of the men in the saloon were dangerous enough to be much of a threat. It couldn't be one of them.Red had to be waiting for some one else.I walked back to the hotel thinking. "What's got enough money in it, to attract a large gang of outlaws? Nothing in Santa Fe had that much money in it."Mary appeared again when the bell rang, as I entered the hotel."Could I get some hot water for a bath?"

"I'll bring you some up in a few minutes.""Tell me where it's at, and I'll get it."Mary smiled a bigger smile at him. Not many men had offered to help her do anything. A stray bullet had killed her husband last year. It had been hard on her since then. She hadn't been interested in another husband.Mary took him back to the kitchen. Susan was finishing supper. I thought she looked mighty pretty. Susan felt hot and sweaty. She didn't feel beautiful."Supper will start in thirty minutes."I picked up a bucket of hot water off the stove. I carried it and my saddlebags upstairs. I put the saddlebags by my bed and the hot water in the bathtub. My room was on the second floor. I had to go back down for a bucket of cold water since the first bucket of water was too hot.Two buckets of water was all Mary would give me since water would be a problem if it didn't rain soon.Susan did not see him come back into the kitchen for the water. She brushed a strand of hair from her face as she turned to get the pan of biscuits.A smile broke across her face when she saw me. I had never seen anyone more beautiful. The strength of my feelings surprised me. I had been taught all the time I had been with the Apaches never to feel or show emotion. It was hard not to show them. I smiled back at her.Mary entered the kitchen and could see that something had gone on between them. She remembered her whirlwind courtship by Doug Estes. They had met and married in three months. She had never regretted it.When the stray bullet from the saloon across the street killed Doug, it had devastated her. If Susan had not been with her, she would have gone crazy. One minute Doug was cleaning off the sidewalk and the next minute he was dead.They had lived in Virginia before they came west. Doug had saved a little money. They thought it was a lot at the time.He had sold their farm and they had come across the country. They had planned to go on to California.They had stayed for the night in the hotel. Susan was eight years old. She had asthma pretty bad. It had cleared up more and more as they came west. In Santa Fe she was free from it.They got to Santa Fe in September. The weather was good.They were tired of traveling. They liked the little town. When the hotel owner said he would sell the hotel for the money they had left, they bought it.It had been a good life until Doug got killed. Now Mary had thoughts of going on to California, or going back to Virginia. The weather got bad in December and stayed that way until May.This made her think of Red, one of their boarders. She didn't really like him and she certainly didn't trust him. He had been staying at the hotel for three weeks and he had been courting Susan.She knew that when Red saw Susan and Tom together, he had a surprise coming. Red made me look a lot better to Mary.I bathed, changed my clothes and was back downstairs just as they started serving supper. Four more boarders were there. Red strutted in about this time.Mary and Susan put platters of pork chops, beans, biscuits and little potatoes cooked in butter, on the table.After the food had been put on the table Mary and Susan sat down with the boarders. Susan sat next to me even though the chair next to Red was empty.She asked me, "Are you planning to stay in Santa Fe?"I told her about my folks and about my capture and the time I spent with the Apaches. I didn't tell it to gain sympathy. I told it so matter of fact that Red snorted a little, when he over heard me."Most men would rather die than live with the Apaches. They would have tried to escape."I looked at Red. "Some men die because they are too soft to live with the Apaches. Other men die because they talk too much and can't back it up."Red started to say something, but he remembered the gambler and thought better of it.Mary got up and brought in the apple pies.Red noticed that I got the first and the biggest piece.He couldn't stand it any longer. He had to try and make me look bad. He told the story of how I had forced the poor gambler out of town, with out giving him time to pack, or get any water.It turned out just the opposite from what he had hoped for. Susan and Mary were looking at me with open admiration.Mary spoke, "Isn't that the man who just shot some one over at the Palace? I bet he deserved to be run off."Susan had not had the opportunity to meet many men she liked. She looked at Tom and thought. "He's the nicest man I have ever met."The look she was giving Tom was apparent to all of them, but especially so to Red.Red was seeing Susan as much as Mary would let him. She let Red talk to Susan in the parlor occasionally. She would only let Susan stay for an hour or so after the supper meal. She never got far from the parlor when Red was there. She didn't trust Red.Red hadn't planned to marry Susan unless he had to. He just wanted her. When the business he was in came to a head, he would take her, use her and leave her for whoever else wanted her.Now Tom was cutting in on him.Red told Susan. "I want to see you tonight after supper."He said it in such a manner, that he was letting Tom know that Susan was his girl."Tom has already asked to talk to me." It surprised me.He hadn't asked Susan but he sure had thought of it.Red's true character came out. "You can't see him, we have an understanding."It was too much for Mary. She flew into Red."Susan has never agreed to anything with you, and she never will."Red jumped up and acted like he wanted to hit Mary. I stood up. Red backed away. “I’ll be back later to pick up my things, I’m leaving!”Mary only said one word to him. “Good.” Susan had never felt comfortable with Red. She felt relief now that he was going. Something about him always bothered her. Maybe it was the way he always looked at her. It was if he was undressing her with his eyes. She was glad her mother had always been close by.Mary had become less satisfied with Santa Fe about three weeks ago, when all the riff raff started drifting in. It seemed that Red had something to do with them.I drank coffee until Mary and Susan cleaned up the kitchen and the dishes. Mary brought a cup of coffee with her, as they joined me at the table in the kitchen.”If somebody comes by and wants to buy this place, I probably would sell. I believe Susan and I would go on to California.”I thought, “I hope no one comes by who wants to buy it.”He had never courted anyone but White Fawn. Morning Star had handled most of that for him. He didn’t know how to court Susan but he was sure going to learn.

Chapter Thirteen

I knew that Susan was the right one for me. Susan, Mary and I talked way into the night. Mary seemed to feel much better about me. She thought, "He is different from most of the western men I have met. He walks with great confidence. He seemed to be soft spoken without any vanity."I told Mary. "Don't sell the boarding house. When I come back after finding my family, I will be able to say more about this." I looked at Susan as I said this. Both of them flushed. It was obvious to Mary, things were moving pretty fast between Susan and me. It had been the same with her and Doug.I told them of my fears that my mother and father might have been killed in Victorio's raid.Mary was grateful that Tom had come along. She shuttered at the thought of Susan with Red. She was horrified that she had been fooled as bad as she had been. Red was a man without substance. Tom was as solid as a rock.Right then she accepted Susan and Tom as being right for each other.Red had fooled a lot of people. He had once been with a gang that called themselves Quantrill's Raiders. He left the gang a couple of months before Cowboy, me and the Cheyenne wiped the gang out.He had been hired to come down to the New Mexico Territory to get as many gunmen as he could for a special purpose. He didn't know what the men were being hired for and he hadn't really met the man who hired him. An Attorney hired him.He had been warned that if he didn't do what he had been hired to do, certain death awaited him. He believed it. He had been in Santa Fe three weeks. He didn't find as many good gunmen as he had thought he would. He turned a lot of them down. Some gunmen were too sorry even for him. He had about fifty of them he could count on.Two of them were coming back into town any day now. They would take care of Tom, the Apache lover.He had given all the men he had hired some supplies and sent them out to a camp a good piece away from town. He didn't want any one in Santa Fe knowing what he was doing, or how many men he had hired. He had been instructed to do it that way.I was up and in the kitchen a few minutes after Mary and Susan got there. All of us had stayed up late talking. Neither he nor Susan had slept much after they went to bed. Both of them had a lot to think about.Susan fixed me some breakfast. Mary told her, "Sit with him for a few minutes. I can fix breakfast for the other boarders."I finished eating. I smiled at Susan. "I'll be back this afternoon."She would have married him then and there if he had asked her. He was the first man she had ever really felt this way about.I walked down to the livery stable. I kept my eyes on all the places for an ambush. I knew Red was a back shooter. I knew I had to handle Red quickly. People like him got worse if you don't take care of them right away.I had planned to saddle Black Devil and ride out before Zeke got there.Zeke saw me coming and already had Black Devil saddled.Zeke told me, "Rumors are Red is going to kill you. Be careful, he won't face you straight out. He will have someone with him.""I've faced a few polecats. A couple more of them won't make any difference. They aren't much when you call their bluff."I got up and in my saddle in one easy motion."Watch out for the one's who have already gone out into the country."

"That's who I'm going to look for. There must be a reason for them to be here in Santa Fe. I would like to find out what they have in mind, before I go and look for my folks."By now Zeke and all the good folks in Santa Fe knew about my ten years with the Apaches. It bothered some of them that I had lived with the Apaches. Most of the people in Santa Fe hated all Indians, but they really hated the Apaches. Santa Fe had a lot of trouble from the Apaches, Comanche, and the Pueblos in it's past. They still had some trouble off and on with the Apaches and the Comanche in the land outside Santa Fe.The tracks were easy to follow. All of them headed in the same general direction. I found a couple of old campfires before I smelled the smoke.I figured that it had to be a large group of men for them to be that careless. I had come about ten miles from town. I left my horse about a half-mile from the place the smoke was coming from. I crawled by two sentries who were looking out into the distance. They didn't expect any one to be close to them.They never knew I could have slit their throats if I had chosen to. I got close enough to hear two men talking."I'll be glad when Jesse Thomas and the other man get here. I'm tired of doing without whiskey and women."

"Me too, Red is back in town having a good time while we're stuck out here.""If Jesse and the other man don't come soon, I'm shucking this place and finding me a good saloon with some pretty women."I still didn't know what was going to happen but I knew it had to be pretty big.Jesse Thomas was a fast gun. Some thought he was the fastest gun, even faster than Wes Hardin, Wyett Earp, or Doc Holliday. I had heard of him in Tucson, Abilene, and Austin. Jesse had robbed a few banks but I had never heard of Jesse associating with this kind of men.A lot of good people thought Jesse had the right to rob banks. I remembered what I had heard about him.Jesse had fought on the side of the Confederacy. He had been away from home. He had a plantation in Alabama. The Fourth Michigan had stopped near his plantation after a battle. They had taken all the horses, hogs and cattle. Jesse's wife had given them almost all the food in the house.Jesse had been good to his slaves. He had released all of them prior to his joining the Southern Army. He wasn't fighting to keep slaves. They were never treated like slaves on his plantation. Most of them chose to stay with the plantation even after he had left.No one knew who started the fire. It was done in the middle of the night. When Jesse's wife, five year old girl, and seven year old boy came out of the plantation to escape the fire, the soldiers shot them and killed them. The plantation burned to the ground. It happened only two months before the war was over. Jesse didn't find out about it until he returned home after the war.When Jesse got home, all he found was ashes. One of the freed slaves had a small garden on Jesse's land. He told Jesse, "I saw the fire, heard something like a shot going off in the house. I was going to get Miss Caroline, young Joseph and Mistress Sarah out when I saw the soldiers shooting at them as they came out of the house. The soldiers thought someone in the house had shot at them. Your family was dead before I could get to them."Jesse was dead too. He just had to keep on breathing for a few more years. He turned to stone. He didn't shed a tear. He wrote out a bill of sale for his land to Old Moses and rode away. He didn't even look back.He had an undying hatred for Yankees, particularly the ones from Michigan. He didn't care whether he lived or died. It gave him an edge over the ones who challenged him to gunfights. He went north to Michigan.He robbed a few Michigan banks. He killed a few Yankee soldiers who challenged him or tried to arrest him. He drifted.His reputation grew as a man who was fast with a gun but who was entirely honest. Nothing was important to him but his honor. He kept his clothes spotlessly clean. He acted the gentleman that he was. He never turned down a challenge.He had nerves of steel. Nothing or nobody scared him. He never back shot any one or backed up from anyone. He didn't have to. He had killed four men who thought they had him boxed in. All he got out of it was a slight bullet wound in his arm.He was coming to Santa Fe.I looked the men over. None of them were very impressive. All of them looked what they were. "Men who had sold their souls to the devil."I made my way back to my horse. At least I knew for sure that Red was hiring for someone else, and that the man he was hiring for, was coming to Santa Fe. He was bringing Jesse Thomas with him.I rode back into Santa Fe and let Zeke have my horse. I smiled when I saw Black Devil nuzzle up to Zeke."Red's got someone waiting for you in the saloon. I don't reckon I would go over there, if I were you."I smiled, "I think I'll go see just what Red has in mind."I had never ducked trouble. I wasn't starting now. I figured the best way to face trouble was to handle it as soon as you knew about it.The man watching for me didn't see me until I was half way across the dusty street. He had been looking for me to come from the alley. I had walked down the street a little and come in between the buildings. The man had been looking for me all afternoon. He started to go in and warn Red. When he looked at me, I shook my head and the man stopped. He wasn't a gun fighter. He didn't want any trouble.

Chapter Fourteen

I walked into the saloon catching Red off guard. He was sitting at a table talking to two men. Red blanched when he saw me enter but he recovered quickly.He smiled as he said something to the men. Both men stood up. I walked on down to the end of the bar so I could keep all of the people in the saloon in my sight.The saloon went silent. Everyone between the gunmen and me moved away. The bartender went down on the floor and crawled over to a safer place.Red had been filling himself with false courage all day. A bottle of whiskey, his second one, sat in front of him.He thought he was safe now that he had two of his fastest guns with him to protect him. I looked both men over carefully. Their cold, unblinking eyes had no fear in them. They were true killers. The one I considered the most dangerous moved with the grace of a mountain cat as he walked up to the bar, stopping a few feet from me. He was tall and thin. His clothes, and guns were spotlessly clean. His black, deadly eyes appraised me.I could tell the man was debating on how fast I was and that he had decided that I was no one to be careless with. It bothered him that he had never heard of me. He knew most of the fast guns. He figured he could beat most of them. He had killed 17 men and he was still alive. That proved something.The other man was a total contrast. He was overweight and dirty all over. His body odor was almost overwhelming. His eyes were red from drinking. They darted back and forth from me to his partner. He was waiting for his signal. He was up on the balls of his feet. He could hardly wait. His hand shook as he held it down by his side. He moved slightly away from Red. I figured I was probably going to get hit at least once by one of the three men. I knew I was still going to kill all of them.Red smiled as he told me. "Tell me again how you were able to live with your children murdering Apaches."I replied. "At least the Apaches are men. They don't bring in their dogs to help them fight. You should have tried fighting your own fights sometimes Red. It might have made a man out of you. Now it's too late, I'm going to kill you." Red nodded his head ever so slightly.The man at the bar was not quite ready. He had underrated me. He thought he had plenty of time. He had not been facing me.He had to turn slightly to shoot me. It got him killed even though he was lightning fast. He lost by a hundredth of a second.He had his gun out and was smiling as he pulled the trigger. His face turned white as my bullet smashed into him, knocking him backwards and wiping the smile off his face.I kept my gun moving toward the second gunman. He had managed to get his gun out and got one shot off.His bullet fanned my cheek as it went by me. He had rushed his first shot. I shot him in the chest. It straightened him up. Red had depended on the two gunmen. Now he had to choose how he was going to die. He could push back and shoot over the table or he could try to shoot under it. It didn't matter which one he chose. He was too slow either way. His face registered the fact he knew he was about to die.My bullet went through the bottle, splattering Red with whiskey as it entered his chest.Red gurgled, spitting up blood and whiskey.The big man was game. He was trying to get his gun back up for another shot at me. My bullet hit him again. It knocked him all the way back against the wall. He crumbled like a rag doll. He slid down the wall. He tried once more to raise his gun. My bullet slapped into him. He twitched a couple of times and lay still.Red was dead, but his body jerked as he slid down in the chair. I didn't take chances. I shot him again. Red didn't jerk anymore. I refilled my pistol with bullets. The men in the bar had never seen anything like it. I had killed three gunmen in less time than the blink of an eye.I went over to Red, went through his pockets. I found a roll of money. I peeled off a couple of twenties, gave it to the shocked bartender. "Get someone to clean up this mess and bury these fellows. Who ever buries them can have the horses and guns that belong to them." I looked through the pockets of the two gunmen. I found fifty dollars on each of them. Red had figured killing me was only worth $100. He should have spent more money. With a couple more good gunmen, they might have been able to do the job.I pocketed the roll of money. I went on over to the boarding house. I didn't tell Mary or Susan about the gunfight.I had felt no more emotion about it, than I would have felt about killing cockroaches. The roaches were better than the outlaws.A couple of newly hired men in the saloon decided they didn't want to be a part of whatever was going on. They had a little money that Red had given them.They finished their drinks and rode out of Santa Fe. Two of the men in the saloon, who had partially earned their reputation just moved on down the street to the other saloons. They would wait for the right time to ambush me.I had finished supper when a delegation of town's people called on me.Zeke spoke first, "We used to have a nice clean town, where women were safe and it was nice and quiet. We want our town to be that way again."Bert joined in. "We don't have any law here. We want you to be our Town Marshall. You're the only one we know who could enforce the law. You proved it when you killed Red and his gunmen."All of the other owners joined in agreeing with him. It was the first time that Susan had heard of the gunfight. Zeke told her the story, as it was told to him.Susan was afraid that Tom might be killed if he took the job. She didn't say this to Tom. He would make up his own mind. Mary was on Susan's side however.I told the men. "I have to go on a short trip. I'll let you know my decision when I get back. I can't make a commitment until I return. I'll be gone about three days."After the men left, I told Mary and Susan, "I'm going back to where my families' cabin is. I've got to find out about my folks."I left before sunrise, with a big package of food they had packed for me.Most men don't travel much at night. Some preferred traveling at night since they thought the Apaches wouldn't fight at night. I knew it was a myth that the Apaches didn't fight at night.It all started because of the giant rattlesnakes that were abundant in the land. The snakes hunted for food at night. Anyone bitten by a 6-foot rattlesnake generally didn't live long enough to tell about it.I rode slowly, always alert. There were too many outlaws roaming around the territory. I stayed off the wagon trail used by Ramon and his men when they came to get supplies for Don Luis and his ranch.I didn't build a fire. I ate the food Susan and Mary had packed for me. It was better than any thing I had packed before.I slept soundly that night although I heard and knew a coyote had circled my camp.I dreamed of White Fawn and Susan. I realized that I had not told Susan about White Fawn. It had not occurred to me that it might make a difference to her until right then. In my dream White Fawn had told me it was all right for me to love Susan also.I had been accepted by Mary completely now, and I felt that I was part of a family again. It was the first time I had felt that way, since the death of White Fawn.I moved on after finishing the rest of the food. The terrain began to look familiar to me. Flashes of memory made me more alert.I remembered the time when my father had shot an antelope over by that tree. Nat and I had found two stray cows over there in that dry wash. The cabin had to be just over the hill in front of me.It kind of shocked me, when it came into view. Several horses were tied in front of the cabin. It had two more rooms added on to it than I remembered.Longhorns were in the corral. All the brush and trees had been cleared from around the cabin for over 200 yards. My Apache training showed. I thought to my self, "That's smart. No one can slip up on them."I saw that it could be defended easily. It did have one flaw. Someone with a buffalo gun could pick off any one who stood in front of the window in the cabin if he was a good shot.A knoll rose sixty feet higher than the land around it. It was over a quarter of a mile from the cabin but an expert rifleman could make the shot.I rode down the slope to the cabin. I kept his hands in plain sight. I didn't know who might live there now. A voice rang out when I was fifty yards from the cabin. "That's close enough. What do you want?"I dismounted slowly so that they could see that I had no intentions of running off or of pulling his gun.I saw a bird fly away from the brush outside the cleared space. Someone had slipped out a side door of the cabin, and gone around me to make sure I was alone.I thought, "They're pretty good at protecting themselves."The voice told me, "Move away from your horse and keep your hands where I can see them."A birdcall sounded out in the brush where the man was. It was the signal that I was alone.The door to the cabin opened and a man with gray hair stepped out. He had a rifle in his hands pointing at my belly. He was a little heavier and had some gray hairs. I recognized him at once. It was my father!My father looked hard at me. I could tell that he did not recognize me at first. Then I saw his face change. He kept looking at me like he couldn't believe what he saw. With a trembling voice he finally asked, "Tom, is that you?"Both of us moved toward each other at the same time. My father grabbed me, lifted me up off the ground, and swung me around. I was more restrained. Apache habits are hard to break. My father kept saying, "We thought you were dead." Jane and Beth came running out of the cabin. They were both crying. I saw that my mother had a little gray in her hair, but otherwise looked the same. She was as pretty as ever.Beth had grown into a beautiful young lady. They were hugging him, along with his father. Tears ran freely down their faces. I had a brief thought, "Why do women cry when they're happy?" Jane noticed how tense and reserved I was. She thought, "What have they done to him, to make him so hard?" Nat, who had slipped out to check on him, came out of the brush and walked over to me. Nat was 18 now and he was a man. He had been a man for several years.He also was a little reserved. He shook hands with me,we looked each other over.

I passed the inspection. I stood 5 feet 11 inches tall. I weighed around 180 pounds.I had two pistols tied low on my hips. I had left the Spenser and my bow on Black Devil. My Bowie knife was stuck down in my belt. I looked like the fighting man I was. Sam liked what he saw. I also had the warrior look. I looked them straight in the eye.In fact Sam said later he had never seen anyone look more like a fighter than I did.Sam figured, after looking me over, the only way you would be able to stop me would be to kill me. He was right.I did like I always did. I analyzed what I saw. My dad gave off the same old feeling of strength and wisdom that I had always felt with him.My mother had some lines in her face, but I could tell that she still had courage and inner strength and was still beautiful.Beth resembled mother, but she had the same firm jaw that Dad had. She could and would hold her own with trouble.Nat stood three inches taller than me. He was thinner. He moved with an easy movement that wasted no motion. It let folks know that he couldn't be trifled with. I could tell that Nat was a man by any standard.Nat had the same feeling about me.Mom grabbed me by the hand and took me inside the cabin.Nat got my horse. Black Devil had been standing still, as he had been trained to do. I watched to see if Black Devil was going to cause Nat any trouble. He hadn't let anyone but Zeke and me near him. To my surprise, Black Devil let Nat rub his neck. Black Devil was getting more sociable. Black Devil followed Nat over to the stable that had been attached to the house.Sam looked at Nat at the same time Nat looked at Sam. Sam shook his head slowly. Nat understood. Sam was saying, "Whatever has happened to Tom has changed him forever. He will never show much emotion again." Nat gave Black Devil some water and feed after he had rubbed him down.

Chapter Fifteen

Jane got out her last apple pie. She had almost run out of everything, especially sugar. She led me into the house. She wanted to put her arms around him and hold him. She sensed that it was not the thing to do. Instead she thought of the pie. Sam and Nat thrived on pies. She remembered that I loved them too.It worked. My mouth watered when I saw the big piece of pie my Mother cut for me. The first bite brought back memories of the happy times I had spent in this cabin.Sam looked at Tom and felt his heart swell. The guilt he had carried with him for the past 11 years left him, making him feel like he would burst. His mind knew that he couldn't have done anything about Tom's capture but his heart wouldn't accept it. Sometimes during those years when Jane had looked at him with tears in her eyes he wondered if she felt that he had let her and Tom down. He felt that he had.As they ate the pie and drank their coffee, Sam told Tom how he, Ramon, Don Luis, and the vaqueros trailed the Apaches to the place where the Apaches had left their horses. He had a hard time talking about Jesus and how Don Luis had looked when they found him, He told me how they felt when they saw the Apaches were not there and the empty feeling in his stomach when Ramon said, "They are gone. They have a two-hour head start on us. No one can catch them now. If Tom is still alive, he may make it back home one day.Sam's voice broke a little. "We found Jesus sitting in a bed of Cholla Cactus. He had been hit in the head. Any of us would have taken his place if we could have. Fifteen more people on Don Luis' ranch had been killed in the raid made by the Apaches."I told them, "I saw Jesus killed because he couldn't keep up. I remember trying to help him and that I seemed to have to run forever. Several times I thought that I would also be killed."Jane caught her breath when I said this.I didn't tell them that Nana had killed Jesus and wanted to kill me also. It seemed to me that it was all a kind of dream and that it had not really happened. I told them how Morning Star nursed me back to health and how Victorio adopted me. I told them how Morning Star taught me the Apache language and customs. I told them how she had become a mother to me. She had lost her only son to the winter sickness when he was seven years old.Sam saw the flash of pain that crossed Jane's face when she heard this. I told them how I had gone through the training required of all young Apache males and how Victorio had trained me in the use of the gun, knife, bow, lance, and war club. Sam felt anger boil up in him when he heard this. He should have been the one to teach me how to grow up to be a man.I explained how the Apaches were similar to the whites in sticking together. When one starved, all of them starved. If there was food it was shared by all. I told them how Victorio spent most of his life guiding the Apaches and how every Apache would give up his life for the rest of the Apaches.They were shocked at some of the things I told them. They had assumed that the Apaches were cruel, evil people who were savages in every respect. Dad could hear the respect that I had for Victorio and his Apaches. I didn't tell them of the hard part of my life with the Apaches. I saw no reason to do so. I tried to explain how the Apaches had been made into the fierce unforgiving people they were by the things that happened to them. They could see that Tom was quiet and yet so strong? He must have gone through many ordeals to have turned out this way."I told them how gradually I had learned to enjoy the Apache way of life, even though it was hard at times. I told them something of Chato, Nana, Quannah, and White Killer.Jane shuddered when she heard the name White Killer.Dad told me some of the things that had happened to them in the 10 years I had been gone. He told me how some renegades and outlaws raided and pillaged some of the small ranches. Two of them had tried it one day when he and Nat were out rounding up some wild mustangs. Sam and Nat knew that I\was not telling everything about my life with the Apaches. They knew by my demeanor that I had been tested many times and that I had not failed. My way of speaking and standing let you know that I was honorable and that I would not back down from anything or anyone.Jane and Beth sensed this too.Jane thought. "What have they done to my son to change him." Sam told about the two men who came to his cabin. "A couple of years ago, two such men rode into the front yard of our cabin. Jane went out to see what they wanted. Beth stayed out of sight. She had her Winchester loaded and ready just in case." Sam smiled as he remembered the story."One of the men asked for some water. You know that in this desert land no one is ever refused water." He continued, "The man who asked for the water got down off his horse. He took his hat off as he talked to Jane. When she turned to go and get the water he grabbed her. The other man, who was still on his horse laughed as he said, Let's take her inside where both of us can enjoy her."Beth took up the story. "I shot him right between his eyes. The man, who was holding mother was surprised too.He had just started to run his hand over mother's body. When he heard the shot, he jerked away from her, trying to get his pistol out. I shot him in the chest. He had an awful look of surprise crossing on his face as I shot him again."Sam and Nat were working a couple of miles away when they heard the shots. They jerked their horses back toward the ranch and rode back as fast as they could. They found Jane and Beth in the kitchen preparing supper as if nothing had happened.She told them, "Take that trash out into the desert and leave it for the buzzards."Beth did have some bad moments after she was by herself but deep in her heart she knew she had done the right thing.Sam looked at Nat who smiled and said, "I hope Jane and Beth don't get mad at us. We wouldn't get any supper for a long time, maybe forever." Sam and Nat did take the trash out into the desert and left it for the vultures.Sam saw me look at Jane and Beth with admiration in his eyes. I told them. "The Apache women would have handled it the same way. They would have taken a longer time to kill the polecats.Sam understood that I meant that they would have tortured the two outlaws a long time before letting them die. The others didn't catch on until later.Sam grinned when he said, "I kind of feel sorry for anyone who comes after us. Jane and Beth are better shots than I am, and Nat shoots better than all of us."They continued talking, bringing me up to date on what had happened to them after I was captured."We received a letter from Elijah telling us that Jane's mother, Jessica, had passed away."Tom had been missing six years when they got the letter. Don Luis had been kind enough to send some of his vaqueros over to run the ranch while Sam, Jane, Nat and Beth went back to Georgia. This time they took a train. They caught it in Santa Fe, rode it to St.Louis, and then on to Atlanta. It only took them six days to get to Atlanta. It took them almost six months to come out here in 1868 in a covered wagon.Elijah passed away four days before they arrived. They said he died of a broken heart. Benjamin Tillman, Elijah's friend and attorney, had put Everett Crenshaw and his wife Sadie running the store until Jane and Sam got there. Jane had good memories of Jonesboro and her father's house but she and Sam had their own home. Their heart was in the New Mexico Territory. She had no plans of ever returning to Georgia to live.She really didn't want to stay in Georgia any longer than necessary so Benjamin arranged a loan for Everett and his wife to buy the store, land, warehouse and the home place of Elijah and Jessica.They got it at a good price. All things considered, it was also a fair price for Jane. She was not rich but she had enough money so that they could live comfortably on it the rest of their lives.Sam also found out that Miss Melonie and Jubal Tate, his old friends, had indeed hit it off and had gotten married. They had sold Miss Melonie's big house and had moved south to Macon where Jubal had come from.Since Sam and Jane had nothing to stay in Jonesboro for, they left after a few weeks. Nat and Beth had enjoyed themselves but everything and everybody seemed to move in slow motion. The people were just as courteous as folks back in the Territory but they didn't have much life in them. They were ready to go home.Jane put her money in the bank and told Benjamin to arrange for her to pick it up in Santa Fe. A letter of credit was issued to that effect. Some things were back to normal in the South.The South was beginning to make a comeback. Cotton was still king. Some of the older plantations had escaped Sherman. Some of the plantations that had been burned were rebuilt. A new class of wealthy people emerged in the South.Carpetbaggers got their hands on a lot of the plantations and a lot of land but they were never included in the old Southern social life that still continued on.When they returned to the ranch, Sam wanted no part of the money Jane had inherited. She did not push it. They still lived off what the ranch made with Sam's contract with the Army. Jane put her money up so that she could help the children if they needed it.I told them about the tribal life of Victorio and his Apaches. I told them of the Apache's struggle to live free and to survive."Victorio, the Shaman and I had a vision showing us that the Apache way of life is about over. They will not fade away without a fight. It will be a good one."I shocked them when I told them. "After I became a warrior and had proved myself, I found myself thinking constantly of a beautiful maiden. She became my wife."For a few seconds he didn't pay attention to the way every one got so silent. He had always told the truth. The Apaches never lied and they accepted everything told them as being part of Ussen's plan for them. He had not been old enough to know how the settlers felt about men who married Indian women.At first Sam was stunned that Tom had married an Apache woman. Beth gasped out loud when she heard the story. Tears filled her eyes. Jane kind of went into shock for a few minutes. She couldn't breathe or speak. She thought, "Tom, my son married to an Apache. Men who married Indian women were called squaw men and sometimes worse than that."Jane looked at Sam. She didn't know how she felt or what to say.Sam calmly shook his head slightly, telling her to be calm. I told them, "The Comanche raided the village of Victorio and in the battle White Fawn, my unborn child, and Red Doe, White Fawn's mother were all killed." I had no emotion in my voice as I told it.Beth got my attention when she started crying openly. Jane also had tears in her eyes. Her kindness had over ridden her hatred of the Apaches for the moment.Sam and Nat stared straight ahead making no sound at all.I told them of the struggles of the Apaches and how everyone was independent if they chose to be so.Jane still felt that all of them should be killed but now there was a little bit of doubt there.She was not alone in her feelings. There was hardly a family in the northern part of the New Mexico territory that had not lost someone to the Apaches. I tried to explain again. "The Apaches have been forced out of their hunting grounds time after time. They have to defend themselves against everyone. They have no other place to go." I turned toward Sam."What would you do if some one came to you and said. "You have to move over to the other side of the mountain. We need this land."Sam's face turned tight for a second. "They would have to kill me. I would not move." Sam realized that Tom had made his case right then. He could feel himself thawing out. He had a long way to go but at least he had the beginning of understanding why Tom liked and respected the Apaches. Tom had made them sound like they were like the settlers.In a blinding flash of understanding Sam knew what Tom was saying.He thought, "They are just like us. All of us will defend our family. They are no different than we are."Even Jane conceded a small part of her hatred of the Apaches. It was the first step of the Davis family in finding peace with the Apaches.Jane calmed down enough to listen to Tom. She would never feel good about the Apaches but she was grateful to them for taking care of Tom and for his safe return.She gave in a little more. "If Tom feels as he does about them, there has to be something good and honorable about them."They talked on and on into the night. They had to catch up on 10 years of information about each other.I told them of Susan and Mary in Santa Fe.I also told them, "I have been offered the job as Marshall of Santa Fe." Sam knew that Tom would be more than able to uphold the law in Santa Fe if he chose to take the job.I told them, "Mary's husband was killed by a stray bullet from the Palace Saloon." An expression of pain appeared on Jane's face as she thought, "What if it had been Sam instead of Doug Estes?" She was so thankful that nothing had happened to Sam. She thought, "How awful it must have been on Mary!"Beth, being romantic was thinking, "I have never heard of anything more sad and beautiful than what has happened to Tom. First he married and loses White fawn. Now he is going to marry Susan." She told me, "You'll have to bring them out here so we can meet them." Jane agreed that they would like to meet Susan and her mother.Sam looked thoughtful when I told him how the outlaws had gathered in Santa Fe and then moved out into the desert.Sam saw the answer first. He said, "I'll bet they are going to make raids on all the ranches in the territory."Nat, who only spoke when he really had something to say, understood it too. "If they burn enough ranches and kill enough people, they will be able to get most of the ranches in the territory for almost nothing."I said, "A man would be a king if he controlled enough of the ranches and land. Jesse Thomas has been hired to help bring all of that about."There was no law available to help the ranchers. The Army had its hands full fighting the Apaches and the other tribes. They would have to do it themselves. The lines that had been in Jane's face since I had been captured were disappearing. She had not spent a single day since then that she hadn't worried and prayed about me. She hadn't known whether I was dead or alive. At that time she didn't know which one would have been better for me. All of the stories had been told, or as much as I would tell them and it was time for us to go to bed.

I told my father. "I'm going to ride out early in the morning. I may beat the heavy rain that is coming."Sam had not noticed any signs that it was going to rain. They all went to bed. I slept on the floor in Nat's room.

Chapter Sixteen

I was up and in the kitchen before daybreak. Sam and Nat were only a few seconds behind me. Sam put on the coffee pot. Jane and Beth got up to prepare breakfast.Nat, Beth and I had slept soundly. Sam and Jane had talked most of the night. Jane could not sleep.She had tears in her eyes when she said. "Tom must have seen a lot of bad things to make him so hard."

"Maybe not," Sam responded. "It may be that the Apaches just don't ever show how they feel. I have heard that about them."Jane was happy to have Tom back under any circumstances. Just about the time to get up she drifted off to sleep lying on Sam's arm. He didn't remove it until she was sound asleep and his arm had gone numb.Sam knew that Tom could take care of himself. He knew one thing for sure. The Apaches had made a man out of him. He was glad that Tom was alive and back home. He had thought several times that Tom might come back but he didn't really believe it. After eating breakfast I told them, "I've got to leave if I'm going to beat the rain. I will bring Susan and her mother with me the next time I come."Jane and Beth would certainly be glad if they came with him when he came back. One of the things they missed was good old women talk. They didn't get to talk with any other women unless they were with Maria Montoya. They would be glad to have more female companionship.Jane and Beth hugged me like they didn't expect to see me again for a long time. It made me tense up. The Apaches left their loved ones without even a wave.Sam shook my hand and walked out to where Nat and Tom's saddled horses were.Nat was going to ride out with Tom and then cut back and circle around the ranch. He had done this almost every morning for years to make sure that no unwelcome visitors were planning to surprise them.I liked what I saw in my brother. Nat looked me straight in the eye when talking to me. I could sense his strength and good judgment. It was the way of the Apaches to look over every one they met to see if they had any apparent weaknesses. Nat didn't have any.Nat nodded at me, "We are glad to have you back. It almost got mother when you were taken. All of us have missed you."I thought for a minute before I replied. "I am sure that it is Ussen that determined the path that I have traveled. I am glad that it has led me back to my family."I continued, "Be careful, my brother, the men who will come to raid this place have no honor. They will not keep their word. Do not believe them and do not show them any mercy. They do not deserve any. However, they will know how to fight."Nat nodded his head.I went on, "I will return, if I can, in time to warn you. Be on the alert though. Something could happen that would prevent me from returning. If I don't get back in time, you take the buffalo gun and fight from the knoll in front of the cabin. They can shoot into the front windows from there."Nat said, "The only way any one but me will shoot from that knoll will be if I'm dead."He wasn't trying to impress me. It was one brave man talking to another.I reached out and clasped Nat's right arm with mine in Apache fashion, "So long my brother, I'll be back as quick as I can."Nat nodded and rode off to make his circle around the ranch. Neither of us looked back.I noticed the clouds forming and knew that I would not beat the rain. I rode Black Devil as fast as I could without punishing the horse or creating danger for him. Black Devil thrived on it. He would rather run than walk. I stopped for a short time in the shade. It was early afternoon. I gave water and dry corn to Black Devil. I ate and continued on. I stayed off the normal trail.Later that evening, about an hour before dark the wind picked up and the rain began to fall. It began to slash down at me. The wind came out of the Southwest and the rain fell in blinding sheets that were occasionally lit up by the lightning strikes around me.I got on the regular trail so that I could make better time. I was reaching for my poncho when a sudden feeling of uneasiness engulfed me. I knew I had made a mistake by getting on the trail even before the shots sounded.I was close to a dry wash. It was some 40 yards to my right. Water was beginning to build up in it.My poncho was stuck. Leaning over to pull it free saved my life.The first bullet cut a furrow on my upper right arm. I continued with my motion and rolled off my horse, pulling my rifle free as I fell. A second and a third shot struck Black Devil in the chest and neck.Black Devil saved my life even as he died. His body shielded me from the five men in the wash.The rain and wind subsided briefly. I heard one of the men in the wash say. "I know I got him. I don't miss from this distance. We had better get out of this wash soon, it's beginning to get a lot of water in it."It had gotten darker. The rain and the wind returned in greater force. It kept me from being seen. I rested my rifle on the dead horse and waited for the lightning to brighten up the sky behind the wash.A bolt of lightning lit up the sky in front of me. I could see the outline of two men framed in the light. I shot both of them.One of them yelled, "I'm hit," before he died. They would not ambush anyone else.I could hear the sound of the other men hollering to each other in the wash. Blood soaked my shirt and pants. I took my bandana and tied it over the wound. It reduced the bleeding.I knew that I would be in a lot of trouble if one of the men decided to slip down the wash and come up behind me. I was about to break for better cover when I heard a noise coming from above the wash. It was about 100 yards from the men. It was a loud hissing sound. It sounded like the pit of vipers that I had almost stumbled into one day. Lightning continued to light up the dark desert sky. During one of the flashes of lightning I saw it coming. It was moving faster than a horse could run. A black wall of water was racing down the wash.The great amount of rain that had fallen had been caught in the canyon above them and had been funneled into the only run off it had.The black water splashed as high as ten feet into the air as it hit the curves of the dry wash. It roared down on the men. Debris was churned down into its black depth and then spewed up to the surface over and over. It was a death trap. The horses knew it. They had already started whinnying and jerking at the reins held by the outlaws. One of the horses broke free. The outlaw holding the horses saw the 10-foot wall of black water come around the bend and race toward him. He opened his mouth to scream. He didn't have time. The water hit them with the force of a runaway stagecoach. One of the outlaws almost got up the bank. It was a futile effort. The raging black water picked him off the bank, along with the rest of the men and the horses and sucked them down into it. It was over in a few seconds. The wall of water didn't give the horses or men time to get any air, it just rolled them over and over on the bottom of the wash taking them with it as it roared away. It took me several seconds before I realized that once again mother nature had proven how unpredictable she was and how fragile people were.With a nod and a thank you to Ussen, I walked over to the dry wash. It still had water several feet deep in it but most of it was gone.Twenty minutes after the rain stopped, the wash would be back to normal again. The desert sand soaked up the water like a sponge.I started to make the long walk back to Santa Fe when I heard a soft whinny from the direction the wall of water had gone. I walked down the wash keeping well away from the edge.Some of the men could have survived. I didn't want to be surprised by them.Seventy-five yards down the wash I saw a brown mare standing on the edge of the wash. It had his head down and was trembling all over. I spoke softly to the horse and approached it. I patted the horse on the neck and talked to it until the horse quit trembling.Somehow the wall of water had picked the horse up, lifted it out of the wash and then put it down on the bank. I had seen many other weird occurrences in my time with the Apaches. I mounted and walked the horse along the dry wash several hundred more yards looking to see if other horses or men had survived. They didn't. I never knew whether the men in the dry wash were gunning for me in particular or just after anyone that came by. I figured that they would have shot anyone, and they had to be some of Red's men.I changed saddles, taking my saddle off Black Devil. I looked down at Black Devil and thought, "You have served me well. You have been like family to me. May Ussen keep you where the deep grass grows, and the sweet water flows. "I had ten miles left to get back to Santa Fe. I rode the dapple brown horse into Zeke's stable. I took the saddle off, rubbed him down with a blanket and put some oats in front of him.I walked over to the boarding house. It was late enough so that even the saloon across the street had closed for a few hours. I knocked on the door to the hotel.Mary came to the door, grumbling as she came. She stopped fussing when she saw me. The rain and the blood from the wound on my arm made me look a lot worse than I was.Susan came up behind her mother. She had a gun in her hand. She gasped as she saw me. She rushed over to me. I calmed her down. "It's only a minor wound."Mary hurried to get an old, clean bed sheet. I told her, "Bring your biggest needle and some coarse thread. If you have any whiskey, bring that too." Susan got a small pan of hot water. I removed my shirt.Both of them were shocked at the scars on his upper torso made from the bullet and knife wounds. Susan cleaned the wound, a four-inch gash, while I told them of the ambush. "I don't know why they ambushed me, but I'm sure they were some of the men hired by Red. Some more men may come into town when they hear that I have killed Red and a couple of his gunmen."I took the whiskey from Mary and poured it on the wound. Jane shuddered and Susan turned white and almost fainted when I took the needle and thread and started sewing up my arm. Susan saw that it was a little awkward since it was my right arm that had the gash on it. I was sewing with my left hand. She took the needle out of my hand. "I'll do that, leave the end open, so that it can drain and will heal quicker." When she finished I poured whiskey on it again before giving the bottle back to Mary.I told them, "Ussen has looked after my family. All of them are alive and well."I told them how I had found them. Tears came in Susan's eyes as I told how my mother and sister had hugged me.Mary snapped her head up when I told them. "I promised to bring you and Susan, the woman I am going to marry back to see them."Mary started to say some sharp rebuttal but bit her tongue after she saw the look on Susan's face.They could see that I had a long day and needed to go to bed.I bathed off and lay down on the bed. I was asleep in seconds.I woke up at the same time I normally did. I had slept less than two hours but it was enough. I had learned that sleeping deeply and soundly for a couple of hours, was enough for any man, or at least any Apache.Susan and Mary were just starting the morning meal when I walked into the kitchen. Except for the slight bulge from the bandage they couldn't tell that I was wounded. I didn't favor that arm. In fact I didn't notice it at all. Mary looked at Susan, "Sit down with him while he eats, I can finish breakfast."I asked Mary to sit with us for a moment. "I need to tell both of you something. When I became seventeen, I had lived eight years with the Apaches. I was an Apache. I thought that I would remain an Apache forever. I took a beautiful young girl to be my wife. It is the way of the Apaches to marry young. We were very happy."I told them of my time with White Fawn. Mary almost jumped up from the table in anger before she controlled herself. Susan was almost in shock, unsure how she felt about it. She felt kind of betrayed! I saw how they reacted and the look that had passed between them.

Mary said. "I can't believe that you were a squaw man."In the west it was an insult, almost the worst thing to be called such a man. It was especially bad to be an Apache squaw man.My eyes hardened. "I know I should have told you before but I didn't think that it would make any difference. I see that it does. I know you have a lot to think and talk about so I will leave. If you wish to talk to me again about this or any other thing we will do so."I had gotten almost to the door when Susan caught me. "It is a shock to me but I know that whatever you have done in the past was right and good. I still feel the same way about you. Yes, I will marry you."Mary's mind was in a whirl. She knew that Susan's mind was made up and that she would not change it. She told me, "I agree with Susan. One day you will have to tell us all about White Fawn."I walked on air as I walked over to Zeke's livery stable.Zeke had opened up an hour earlier.I told him. "I will take the Marshall's job, with a few conditions."Zeke spit a stream of tobacco juice at a scurrying bug and replied, "You can have it under any condition you want. Let's go over and talk to McGregor."McGregor owned the big mercantile store and was by far the richest man in Santa Fe and if the truth was known, he probably was the one who made most of the big decisions about Santa Fe. He had recognized the need for water and had started talking of digging a ditch from the Sangre De Christo(Blood of Christ) Mountains above Santa Fe. A lot of people laughed at him but eventually it was done and Santa Fe grew because the ditch caught the run off from the melting snow and ran it into a reservoir made to hold it.On the way over I asked Zeke, "Who owned that big dapple brown I rode in last night?"

"Belongs to a no account named Bart O'Conner. He mistreats that horse sometimes."I told him, "He won't mistreat that horse or any horse ever again."Zeke looked at me with a twinkle in his eye. "Good riddance! You're a man after my own heart."

Chapter Seventeen

Zeke took me over to McGregor's Mercantile. It was an adobe building that ran in all directions. McGregor had expanded his store each of the ten years he had been in Santa Fe.McGregor was a likable man. He kind of stood out for some reason. He knew the name of every customer who traded with him. He knew their family. He helped many a traveler and settler down on their luck. He did it quietly. McGregor was the unofficial mayor of Santa Fe. He was not very big in size, but everyone listened when he spoke. He always cut to the bottom line. He didn't waste many words.He smiled when Zeke told him that we wanted to talk to him.He looked at me. "We used to have a nice town, still do. However we are growing so fast we are attracting a lot of undesirable people. We need a lawman to make sure we do not turn into a town like Tombstone."

"We will pay you $100 a month and you can have all the fines you collect. You are free to arrest whomever you will. Do what you think best."

"Where will we put the ones we arrest?"McGregor looked around, thought a minute and said. "I have two rooms behind the store that are vacant. One room does not have any windows. It has an oak door between the two rooms. That will work pretty well as a jail." He showed the rooms to me. They were dirty, still had some boxes and old furniture stored in them.McGregor told me, "I'll have one of my clerks clean the rooms up for you today."I had already been thinking of what I needed to do. I asked McGregor, "Can you make me some signs that say?" No guns allowed in Santa Fe." Pistols will be left on saddle horns, rifles will be left in their saddle boots."McGregor smiled, "That's a good idea, if you can enforce it. Come back in two hours and I'll have the signs ready for you."Since I had to wait two hours and it was almost noon, I went back to the boarding house to eat.Mary and Susan were not surprised that I took the job. Susan thought I would. I spent a couple of hours with them and went back to McGregor's and got the signs. I put the first one up outside the saloon across the street.Bill Jackson, the bartender didn't want me to put up the sign."It's 2:30. I start enforcing this at 4 o'clock." I spent the next hour and a half putting up signs all over town, especially at the ends of the street where the gunmen entered the town. It was a little after four when I finished. I knew that I would be tested in the Palace Saloon. I went back to it.I noticed the horses in front of the saloon. All of them had pistols hanging on the saddle horns except two. I paused at the door, letting my eyes adjust to the gloom before I went in.Two burly cowboys were sitting at one of the tables. I saw Bill Jackson wink at one of them. Bill had his hands below the bar.I waved him from behind the bar, watching him carefully. When Bill was clear, I walked over to the two men. "Did you guys read the signs telling you that no guns were allowed in Santa Fe?" Ben Cobles looked me over. I didn't look like much to him. Ellis Woodham, his partner, had the same opinion. They made the mistake of letting me get in too close.Ben grinned a little as he said. "We don't read so well; maybe you can read it to us." He was putting on a show for his partner, Ellis.Ellis giggled a little. "We don't obey signs anyway." Ben Cobles started to push back his chair to reach for his gun. In one swift motion, I pulled my gun and swatted Sam on the top of his head. I continued the motion and caught Ellis on the side of his face with the barrel.It stunned Ben, but he was not out so I hit him again. I knocked him out of his chair. Ellis grabbed his face. His nose and jaw were broken. He kept spitting broken teeth out.I reached over and took his gun. I walked over to Ben, never taking my eyes off Bill the bartender. I figured Bill for a man that kept a gun hidden on him. Bill didn't move. He had seen me in action two times. That was enough for him.Ben was trying to sit up. I took his gun from him. I looked in Ben's shirt pocket. I found $100 there. Ellis had the same amount tucked into his shirt. I told the bartender, "I fine each of them $100 each for disturbing the peace."I heard a noise behind me at the door. I spun and was about to shoot when a familiar voice rang out. "I knew it had to be you. There can't be two white Apaches in this neck of the woods."It was Cowboy, who grinned and said, "I thought I might have to give you some help with these broken down cowhands. It's them that need the help. I should have known better."Cowboy explained how he had been in the Mexican Cantina down the street when a man told him of the lawman who had lived with the Apaches and had recently killed three gunmen.I turned to Bill Jackson. "I see the price of killing me has gone up. When these two men come to their senses, tell them I said for them to get out of town and never come back. The next time anyone attacks me in this saloon, I'm going to hold you personally responsible. I'm going to kill you."Bill Jackson blanched a shade paler than he already was. He was a bartender, not out in the sun much. He didn't own the saloon, although everyone in town thought he did.I walked over to where Cowboy was standing and shook hands with him.I asked him, "What's the matter, is Texas too tame for you?"Cowboy grinned as he and I walked outside. "I went back to New Laredo and found Rosita. Everything was mighty good, just not what I had been dreaming of. The next day I found out that Rosita had not told me everything."What did she leave out?"

"She forgot to tell me that she had married the Sheriff. The Sheriff returned home that night and I made a strategic retreat. I crossed the border about thirty minutes in front of him and his posse. I'm glad I got to see Rosita again. It was worth the trip. I think the Sheriff has more woman than he or any one man can handle."I asked Cowboy if he wanted a job, if he wanted to be my deputy. Cowboy laughed and said, "It would be good to be on this side of the law for a change." He accepted.I showed him the jail. It had been cleaned up. McGregor had put a desk in one room and a cot in the other room to be used as a cell. It was not much but it would do.I introduced Cowboy to McGregor, and took him back to the boarding house to meet Mary and Susan.I was surprised to see Cowboy so nervous and shy when he met them. He had never been that way before around women. He later told me, "I don't know how to act around good women since I have only known one other good woman in my life. She was my mother."Susan and Mary couldn't do enough for Cowboy when they found out he was my best friend. Mary didn't even give him the lecture she had given me and everyone else who stayed with them.I told Mary, "I would trust Cowboy with my gun, my money and my life. I would trust him with everything but Susan."Mary laughed. Susan blushed and Cowboy squirmed, his face turning red. I thought about the men in the saloon. I told them that I would be back in a few minutes. Mary and Susan had Cowboy surrounded. They couldn't do enough for him. He enjoyed it but he was having a hard time trying to figure out what to say to them. It almost floored him when Susan said that she and I were going to get married.He thought to himself, "How lucky can one man be. Susan is pretty and really nice. She is the kind of woman any good man would like to have."I went over to the saloon. Ben Cobles and Ellis Woodham were sitting at one of the tables. Ben kept shaking his head, trying to remember what had happened to him. He was trying to decide what he needed to do next.Ellis had a hankerchief pressed to his nose and mouth, trying to stop the bleeding. He wasn't doing much good. His broken nose and broken jaw were beginning to send spasms of pain through his face and head. Both of them had a glazed look in their eyes.Bill Jackson looked at them with disgust. He had figured them to be tougher. Bill blanched a little when he saw me come in.I asked the two men, "Who hired you to kill me?" Neither man answered. I did not expect them to. Even the outlaws had some code of honor.They did understand it when I told them, "Get on your horses and get out of town. If you're not gone in ten minutes, we'll bury you here!"It took them seven minutes. They left their pistols with me. Neither man looked back. They knew they had been lucky. I could have killed both of them easily.Things slowed down after that. The news got around. The traffic, that had come and gone in the Palace Saloon, almost dried up. Even some of the town regulars moved on down to the Mexican Cantina on the other side of town.Rumors of men coming out the cantina on the other side of town persisted. One rumor had it that one day Jesse Thomas was coming in to get me.I decided that I had better take Mary and Susan out to see my family during the lull. I knew trouble was coming. I could feel it.I talked to them that evening. "In the morning I am going back to see my folks. Would you like to go with me?"Both of them wanted to.It was a couple of hours before sundown when I noticed three horses in front of the Palace that didn't have guns hooked to their saddle horns.The word had gotten round and I did not have to enforce the law too many times before folks began to respect it. I had put two drunken cowboys in jail until they sobered up. I had run two more would be bad men out of town. All in all it had been almost peaceful.Cowboy took a Scatter Gun, a shotgun with about half the barrel sawed off. It gave a spread of buckshot that would cover a man easily.From 20 feet you couldn't miss. It would blow a man to pieces. Cowboy timed his entrance through the back door to coincide with me coming in the front door. The three men standing at the bar were not afraid. That was obvious. All of them had their guns tied low on their legs. One of them had two pistols hung with their butts forward. He was a cross draw man.Some one said Wes Hardin started the cross draw and he thought it was faster. I didn't know about it. I had never seen it before. The three men were obviously good with their guns.They automatically spread out so that they could be in position for both Tom and Cowboy. Two of them looked at the third man for instructions.The man they kept looking at was tall and thin. He was enjoying the tenseness. All of them could sense the danger generated by the people in the saloon. A lot of folks were going to get killed if someone drew his gun.The man smiled easily. Every movement he made was graceful. Tom felt the sureness of the man. He would be the most dangerous by far. The other two were good but they couldn't hold a candle to their leader. And they knew it."My guess is that you're the town Marshall."My smile was just as big as the thin man's was. "That's a good guess. The fellow with the Scatter Gun is my deputy. My guess is that you fellows didn't see the sign about not carrying a gun while in town."One of the two men with the thin man flushed and started to cuss. He was silenced by a wave of the hand by the leader. The man smiled even more. "I'm Jesse Thomas. I wanted to see the man good enough to kill three good men at one time."I knew who he was. "I'm Tom Davis. I figured you to be Jesse Thomas. The three men I shot were really not that good. I have seen better." Jesse laughed. He was impressed by my candor. He was enjoying himself.I laughed also. "I'd appreciate if you fellows will oblige me by putting your guns on your saddle horns."Jesse looked him over very carefully. He turned to the two men with him. "Boys I believe the man is serious about his sign. I do believe that he can enforce it too."He nodded his head at one of the men with him. "This is Kyle Cates and this other fellow is Paul Bideau."Both men had earned their reputations as fast gunman. Bideau was the most stable of the two. Cates was considered to be crazy. Both of them were men who would stop at nothing unless forced to. They didn't respect laws, women, or religion. All they respected was brute force.Cates could hardly contain himself. "You don't look so tough to me."Jesse shook his head, "Cates, your bad temper and bad judgment are going to get you killed one day. This could be that day. The Marshall would kill you before you got off one shot. It might solve some of my problems if I let you go on and fight him."He looked back at me. "And I might learn something about you when I see you kill him. A gun fight between me and you might be real interesting."I stood easy. "Could be Jesse. I wonder why you're on the side of this riff raff. I never heard about you being associated with back shooters before."Both of the men with Jesse stiffened. They were watching Jesse. They figured he was going to start a gunfight any second now.Jesse declined. He told me, "Some day we may talk about it. If either of us make it through what's coming."I shook my head at him. "I hope what you're doing is worth dying for."Jesse's face changed. "Dying is easy. It's the living that's tough. Come on boys, let's get out of here before one of you lose your head and gets us all killed by the Marshall and his deputy."I liked Jesse. I saw a man with class and character written all over him.I decided to try to get to him. "When you decide to quit this gang of outlaws, come see me." Jesse smiled, "One day I may do just that."

Chapter Eighteen

Cowboy stood at the corner of the building, watching them ride away. With a sigh of relief he joined me on the porch."Looks like something big is going on."I responded. "I think someone is going to try to take over a good portion of the territory. My father told me of some raids on some of the smaller ranches. I think it's about to begin here in Santa Fe and at my father's ranch. Don Louis Montoya has a big ranch and I believe they will hit him too."Cowboy looked at me, wondering how I knew this. "Wonder who's behind all this? It's got to be someone richer and smarter than any of these outlaws we've seen, with the exception of Jesse."I smiled when Cowboy said that. "Jesse is some fellow. He would be someone to ride the river with. Something isn't right about him being with those skunks."

"Think about a gun fight between you and Jesse. Man, I could sell a thousand tickets to folks who would want to see that."

"I hope it doesn't come to that. I'd hate to be killed by Jesse and I wouldn't feel good about killing him. However, Ussn will make the decision on what happens between us. It is as it should be."I felt that there would be several days of peace before the fight started. As we walked back to the boarding house, I told Cowboy, "In the morning I'm taking Mary and Susan out to see my folks. We'll be gone about five days. If trouble starts before I get back, get Zeke to round up some men to help you."Cowboy grinned. "Partner, I can handle most of the things by myself." I knew he could. Cowboy had already proven himself to me.Mary, Susan, Cowboy and I talked about the trip they were making the next day.I found out that Mary and Susan could ride.Mary left them saying, "I've got to get something ready for us to eat on the way."I went down the street to Zeke's stable to get the right horses for them. Cowboy kept sneaking peeks at Susan, who smiled at him. He couldn't help noticing how pretty she was. He was deep in thought about how lucky Tom was when she startled him."Do you have someone waiting for you back home?"Cowboy flushed as he remembered Rosita and the way he had left in front of her husband's posse. "No mam, I'm afraid I'm not as lucky as the White Apache, Tom, I mean."

"Tell me how you met Tom."Cowboy had finished the story when I walked in."Zeke's got you and Mary some good horses. I figured we'd leave early in the morning."Mary and Susan were up and raring to go when I got to the kitchen. They had fixed their breakfast and packed enough food to feed an army.We pulled out at the crack of dawn. I kept a slow pace for the first few hours. My father's ranch was about 65 miles from Santa Fe. I kept my eyes on the ground in front and on both sides of me. I read the trail both ways at the same time. I kept my eyes moving. It is the way the Apaches survive. The Apaches were seldom ambushed. The birds or insects gave away the ambush. Sometimes their natural instincts made them aware of it. Neither Mary nor Susan noticed my watchfulness.We stopped for lunch at a small spring. Mary and Susan made a picnic out of it. Both of them were getting sore from riding. They tried not to show it. Mary got the fried chicken and bread from the bag on her saddle. I had never eaten this good on any of my journeys. I never relaxed. I kept my eyes moving across the landscape around me. I knew the outlaws had come this way. I saw many sets of horse prints on the trip. I kept us off the ridges and gradually worked my way in a general direction toward the ranch. Neither of them knew that I was worried. Twice I had considered asking them to quit talking. We covered about half the distance before stopping for the night. We could have traveled further but I wanted to cut back and see the place the outlaws were hanging out. We were several miles beyond it. I thought the ladies were safe now.I found a place off the trail. It was sheltered on three sides by large boulders. The single opening limited the entrance to only one person at a time. I found enough wood that had been dry a long time to keep the small fire burning until I got back. The dry wood had very little smoke coming from it. Someone would have to be close to smell it.Mary and Susan each had a repeating rifle. I had made sure of that. I told them, "If anyone comes in the entrance of the rocks without whistling like a jay, shoot him. I will be back around midnight."They didn't see him leave. One second he was standing there, and in the next second he was gone.Mary looked at Susan, "That's down right spooky." She wasn't quite sure she felt good about being left by themselves. She did know that if trouble came they would do right well facing it. They always had.I rode quickly, cutting straight toward the outlaw's camp miles away. The reflection from their campfires could be seen a long way from the fire. I was more afraid of bumping into an Indian than I was of the outlaws seeing me. I left my horse a half-mile from the camp and slipped past the outer guards easily.I snaked my way on my belly up to the edge of the camp. I scanned the camp looking directly at each outlaw. I wanted to remember each one of them.Four men sat at one of the campfires. I crawled over closer to them. I was close enough to hear their conversation.Jesse Thomas was one of the men. I could tell that Jessie was mad. Kyle Cates sat next to Jesse. I didn't know the third man. The fourth man had his back to me.The hairs on the back of my neck bristled. I heard the man say to Jesse. "What's all the fuss about? So Kyle and Quirt had a little fun with the rancher's wife before she grabbed a gun and made them kill her."They both had smiles on their faces. Jesse got even madder,

"You call that a little fun. Black Jack, this is not what you told me about. You told me we were going to take land away from Yankee carpetbaggers. None of these folks had any thing to do with the war."

Tom knew who the fourth man was before the man turned to face Jesse. It was Black Jack Ketchum!I saw Jesse struggle to control himself. Jesse wouldn't mind dying if he could take the three men with him. He knew he had to be smart about it. He would have to play along with them to make sure he got to settle up with Black Jack, Kyle and Quirt.Jesse nodded, "I didn't sign on to make war on women and kids, but maybe sometimes it's necessary."Black Jack relaxed. For a minute he thought he was going to have to get one of his men to shoot Jesse in the back. "Day after tomorrow, most of it will be over. We'll hit the Davis ranch and the Montoya ranch. The rest of them will be easy pickings. We have about 75 men now. It ought to be more than enough. Especially if we trick them."I had heard enough. I was tempted to go on and shoot Black Jack and Jesse. I figured someone might get me. My father and Don Luis Montoya would not know of the plot to take their ranches. I would get my chance to meet Kyle, Quirt, and Jesse again. Mostly I wanted to face Black Jack. I knew that Black Jack was totally void of any sense of good or decency. He needed killing.I carefully made my way back to my horse and then back to the place I had left Susan and Mary. I had been gone hours longer than I had intended. They would be worried about me.It was about three in the morning when I reached their shelter in the rocks. I made the call of the Jay as I entered the rocks.It was a good thing that I did. I heard the rifle in Mary's hands being cocked."One more second and I would have shot you." Mary shuddered to think what she had almost done.I smiled. In a teasing manner I told her, "I should have told you to cock the rifle before you heard someone coming. I could have gotten off several shots at you before you fired."Mary and Susan both paled a little. It was the small things that got you killed in the west.I told them what I had found out. I told them to wake me after one hour and we would continue on to my father's ranch.Almost to the minute my eyes popped open and I got up. Mary had gone to sleep. Susan was giving me one more minute before she woke me up. She had been too excited to sleep anyway.They ate the rest of the food Mary had packed. The cool spring water was refreshing. The night air was cool. It was amazing how low the temperature dropped during the night.The dark night sky was lit up with millions of stars. I caught a whiff of the smoke from the outlaw's campfires. It was a good thing for them that the outlaws had so many men or they would probably have some Apache visitors.I knew that I could have killed many of the outlaws with just a few men. We would have crawled up on the camp, opened fire on the men in the camp and melted away. It would have created chaos among the outlaws. The Apaches and I would have picked them off one at a time later.In fact that was exactly what I had in mind for them.It didn't take us long to move out. I cautioned the ladies about talking. I told them that sound carries a long way in the desert. We rode faster now. We didn't ride fast enough to wear the horses out or cause any real hardship to Susan and Mary. I wanted to get to my father's ranch by noon if they could.We didn't quite make it by noon. We got to the ranch a little after four. Susan and Mary were worn out. Both of them were sore and tired. Neither of them complained about it.I yelled at the cabin as we approached it. Jane and Beth came out the door when they recognized me. Both of them had their rifles with them.I introduced them to each other. The women looked each other over as all women do. I asked Jane where Sam and Nat were. "They're working a little south of here." I rode out to find them.

Jane took Susan and Mary into her home. She told Beth, "Make them some hot tea while I get them some food." She showed Susan and Mary where the small barrel of water used for bathing was. She gave each of them a washrag and towel she had been saving for such a purpose. Susan had put some hot water in two small basins for them. They could add enough cold water to it to suit themselves. Jane and Beth left them so they could perform their absolutions in private. They knew that Susan and Mary would feel better after some of the dust from the trail had been cleansed from them.When I returned with Sam and Nat the ladies were having a good time together. It was almost like they had known each other a long time. Maybe the fact that they had their love for Tom in common helped some. At any rate Susan and Beth were talking a mile a minute and Jane and Mary were not far behind.Neither of the women had talked to an over abundance of female companionship since they had been out west. They had a lot to catch up on.I looked at the women, realizing what would happen to them if the plans of Black Jack Ketcham succeeded. It turned my stomach. I had to prevent it. I knew what I had to do. I would take the war to the outlaws. Sam sent Nat to warn Don Luis Montoya of the plans of the outlaws and about when they could expect them.It was the outlaws who had a surprise coming!We had time to arrange a surprise party for the outlaws who were going to raid them. Mary and Susan would stay at Sam's ranch while I delayed the outlaws by ambushing them. At least I could kill Black Jack and Jesse.Sam directed the ladies. "Jane, cook enough for a couple of days." Mary volunteered to help her. Beth and Susan tore up some old sheets and boiled them in case they needed bandages. Sam took the horses and cattle up to another range. All of their personal horses were brought into the room used as a corral. Sam had six rifles loaded and placed at the windows. Pistols were placed along side of them. Jane got out all of her medical supplies. Susan and Mary were shown how to load and shoot the guns. Beth and Jane already knew this. Beth had already killed two men. They oiled and cleaned all the guns. I told Dad, "Watch out for the knoll in front of the house. If I don't get back in time Nat can sit up there and pick off a lot of them."All the windows had shutters with gun slots in them. They closed and bolted them. I went out and got some herbs to boil in case one of them got shot. Jane put the herbs in a pot and boiled them like I told them to do. They smelled awful. I told them, "These herbs will stop the pain if you drink the juice and they will stop infection if you put it on a wound." I knew this to be true because Victorio and Morning Star had saved my life with them.

They were safe at least until late the next day and probably the day after. All of them went to bed early. Sam took the first watch. I heard Nat coming just before he signaled that he was back.Don Luis wanted to send some men over but Nat had told them what I had said. "We don't need help. We can take care of them." Don Luis was looking forward to the attack. He needed something to break the monotony. Nat was greeted with hugs from the ladies. He blushed some. Nat had been seeing the daughter of one of the vaqueros who worked for Don Luis. They were almost serious about each other.I looked at the ones in the cabin and said, "When they come, stay in the cabin. They will try to trick you into coming out. Shoot them. Show them no mercy. If worse comes to worse, don't let the women be taken alive!"The harsh words startled them. Even Sam, who had already decided the same thing was surprised. Tom changed right before their eyes. He put the two pistols on. He put his Bowie Knife in its scabbard. The bow and arrows were hung on his back. He picked up his 50 Caliber Spenser and his Winchester Repeater. He put his war club in his belt. His eyes turned as hard as a mid winter night. He was ready. They were astounded at the change in him. It scared Susan.I knew where I would ambush them, five miles from the place the trail split. One trail went toward Don Luis' ranch and the other led to Sam's ranch. A ledge was not far from the trail. They had to come by there to raid either ranch. I would kill Black Jack, Jesse and as many more as I could before slipping away to hit them again down the trail. I would even up the odds some. It would let them know they could be killed. Raiding the ranches was not going to be easy. I hardly noticed how quiet the women had gotten before I rode out.

Chapter Nineteen

I knew the outlaws had to be close by. The dust kicked up by their horses had been visible for 25 minutes. The outlaws rode with great confidence. Being part of such a great number of fighting men made them think they were invincible.I picked Black Jack out with ease. He rode in front. They were so confident in themselves that they didn't even send out flankers or scouts. Only two of the men concerned me. Jesse Thomas and a half-breed called Turkey Joe. The half-breed said that he was part Blackfoot. What ever he was he could track. Jesse could too although he wasn't as good as Turkey Joe or me.Jesse was not in front. Neither was Turkey Joe. Too many years of fighting had cured them of being stupid enough to be out front and the first one to get killed.I waited patiently. I thought they might be on to me when I saw Jesse and Turkey Joe look directly at the ridge and keep looking at it. I waited until they were 500 yards out.Black Jack had lived many more years than he should have by being lucky and sacrificing his men in order to survive.I lined up my sight on Black Jack's chest. I allowed eight inches for the wind that was blowing from left to right. I slowly pulled the trigger. Black Jack jerked his horse around to talk to Jesse.The 44 cal. bullet creased his coat as it burned by him. The sound of the rifle was a split second behind the bullet.Jeb Scott who was right behind Black Jack took the bullet in his stomach. Bill Regan who was behind Jeb Scott was hit in the leg when the bullet went through Jeb. It shattered Regan's kneecap. Jeb Scott had a half-inch hole in his stomach and a two-inch hole in his back where the bullet exited.Black Jack's horse started bucking. So did Bill Regans's. I emptied my Winchester into the mob of men trying to get off the trail. Jesse and Turkey Joe rode off to the side into the brush. One of my bullets hit Turkey Joe, knocking him out of his saddle. It ended his career as an outlaw. It busted his hip crippling him forever.Six men were killed including Jeb Scott. Four more were wounded. Two of them were out of action for good. The other two were not so willing to go along right now.By the time the men quieted their horses and got their rifles I was long gone. The bullets from the outlaws raked the ledge. Jesse watched the action with a smile on his face.Black Jack finally got the men to stop shooting after Jesse told him that it was useless, that the man they were shooting at was gone.Black Jack was livid. How did any one know they were coming? All of the 75 men had been with him all the time.Jesse told him, "I've got a feeling that our friend the Marshall is a lot smarter than we had figured." It made Black Jack mad. He began to cuss.Jesse let him vent his anger some and then told him, "Let me take Quirt and Kyle with me and I'll see if we can't turn the tables on him. You wait here for a while and if we get him, we will fire three shots."Black Jack trusted Jesse. He might be the only man he had ever trusted. If the truth could be known he wished that he were like Jesse. "Go ahead, we'll wait until we hear the shots." He thought to himself, "I've still got 67 men, it ought to be enough to take two ranches."Jesse had picked the two men who had murdered Rancher Spangler and his wife.Jesse turned off the trail. I stopped at my second place of ambush. It was a small draw with a back exit. I would be a lot closer to them this time.Jesse rode out a mile or so before he cut back toward the trail. Without knowing it he picked almost the exact place that I had picked.I watched them come. Jesse stopped, not more than 50 yards from me. I could tell by their actions that they didn't know I was there.Jesse got down off his horse and examined the ground. He told Kyle and Quirt to do the same. Kyle had something bothering him but he got off his horse like Quirt did.Jesse stepped back another step, dropped his hand next to his gun. "Tell me again how you polecats ambushed the rancher and then had fun with his poor defenseless wife."It took Quirt a second longer to catch on than it did Kyle.Kyle looked hard at Jesse. Maybe Jesse wasn't so tough after all. If Jesse picked Quirt to shoot at first, he would be able to shoot Jesse. He always figured he could beat Jesse any way.I watched the scene with interest. Jesse wasn't as bad as I had thought.Kyle took a step sideways. So did Quirt, who was scared to death. Why had he got into this in the first place? He had the feeling that he was going to die.Kyle tried, "Make your move," as he grabbed for his gun. He had figured he might get a jump on Jesse.Jesse put his first bullet in Kyle's shoulder. His gun flew out of his hand. Quirt was almost crying as he went for his gun.It never cleared leather. The pain in his chest where the bullet hit him increased briefly and he was gone.Kyle couldn't believe it. Neither he nor Quirt had got off a shot. Jesse shot him in the stomach. "It's going to take you about an hour to die. I hope you remember the rancher and his wife on your way to hell. "Kyle tried to get his gun out but couldn't. Jesse took his gun and Quirt's and turned to walk off.A voice came from behind him, "I'm glad to know that I was right about you."Jesse spun, drawing his gun at the same time. He almost fired before he recognized me. I stood at ease with my hands out in front of me. "That could have got you killed," Jesse said quietly."Not with a good man like you. I knew you always looked before you fired." I walked toward him. Black Jack heard the three shots and rode on toward the two ranches. He believed that whoever had ambushed them was dead. Jesse had seen to it.I held out my hand to Jesse. "You want to help us clean up this mess."Jesse smiled as broad as he could. "I would be delighted. It's the first time I feel good about this."I wanted to get back to the ranch ahead of the outlaws. Jesse and I took the back trail getting back to my fathers ranch. We were about half an hour in front of the outlaws. On the way Jesse told how he had met up with Black Jack. He had been in Independence, Missouri when Black Jack came through recruiting gunmen to fight some Yankee land grabbers in the New Mexico Territory. He never fully believed Black Jack but he was tired of running. He wanted to settle down his last few years and The New Mexico Territory sounded fine. Black Jack lived high, took care of the men he recruited and kept all of his promises to Jesse. In his heart Jesse knew that something wasn't right about Black Jack. It became apparent the night he heard them talking about the raids on the small ranches. Jesse had been in the Territory only one week when he heard about the ranches. He vowed to kill Black Jack, Kyle Cates and Quirt before he left. He had one of them left, Black Jack.

Chapter Twenty

The women were impressed with Jesse when we got back to Sam's ranch. His genuine southern manners and tall good looks appealed to all of them. Even Jane felt a quickening of her pulse. Jesse represented all of the good things of the South. He was good looking, had a good sense of humor, and was always saying and doing the right thing. When he kissed Beth's hand she almost swooned. Nat returned from scouting. They were ready for the outlaws. They discussed the best way to defend the ranch. It was a tribute to Nat that they listened to him and agreed with him that all the horses needed to be taken a good distance from where the battle would be. I told Jesse that I was going to fight outside. Jesse elected to do the same. We decided that Jesse could do the most good defending the rear of the cabin. The outlaws were certain to attack there. I told him that the rear of the cabin had some rocks off to one side that would offer him some protection. I figured that some of the outlaws would try to slip up behind the rocks to attack the rear of the cabin. Nat, Sam, Jane, Beth, Susan, and Mary would fight from inside the cabins. I went up to the ridge in front of the cabin. I climbed to its highest point. It gave me a good view of the killing zone. Jesse had a Spencer 15 shot repeaters and two pistols. I had my Winchester, bow and my buffalo rifle. I also had two pistols. A few minutes after we took up our position the outlaws got there. They were expecting little or no resistance. They didn't know that we were waiting for them.I watched them ride by below me.Glenn Elliott, one of Black Jack's Lieutenants, noticed the cleared brush from around the cabin. He knew it gave the people inside a good, clear killing field. Black Jack had given Glenn 30 men to take the ranch. Black Jack took the rest of the men with him to take Don Luis' ranch.Glenn sent three of his men forward. He thought that someone would come out of the cabin to talk to them. It would give them a chance to kill whoever came out.When no one came out, the three outlaws rode closer to the cabin. Sam had his rifle trained on Gimpy Brown, the spokesman.Gimpy had thought it would be easy. He decided he could frighten the people in the cabin into giving up. Maybe they wouldn't have to kill the women until later.He yelled out to the people in the cabin, "Come on out and we'll spare you. You can ride off. All we want is your ranch. If you don't come out, we'll burn your cabin down with you in it." They did not plan to spare anyone in the cabin. They didn't want any witnesses left alive.Sam heard enough. His three shots rang out and all three men fell out of their saddles. Glenn Elliott yelled at his men, "Take cover. We'll blast them out."The outlaws pulled back into the brush beyond the edge of the clearing. Since I was much higher than they were, I could see most of the men as they scattered. I began to shoot slowly but surely. It was hard to miss with the rifle. I killed six of them before they caught on and pulled further back.Glenn Elliott was a pretty good soldier at one time. If you had asked when and where he went wrong he couldn't tell you. He split up his forces. He sent five men to the rear and five on each side of the cabin.He, Rafe and Henry would go after the one who had shot from the ridge. Three men left would follow them up the ridge to back them up. He had lost 9 men and they had not seen anyone yet.The three men slipped slowly up the ridge toward me. They spread out so they would cover more ground. They thought it was safe. The three trailing men came up even slower.

I came down to meet them. Glenn led out. He put Rafe on one side of him and Henry on the other. They had fought many battles together. Glenn Elliot had never thought of dying in "The War Between The States." For some reason it ran through his mind now. Something was telling him. "You had better get out of here." He ignored it.If one of them drew fire, the other two would fire where the shots came from. It wouldn't take long to clear the ridge.I sat behind a small cluster of rocks. I could see one of the men just back of the leader raise his head occasionally to look for me. The next time he raised his head I shot him with my bow.Glenn heard the twang of the bowstring. He whispered to Rafe. "They must be low on ammunition for him to be using a bow."I spotted Henry through the brush. Henry crawled right into the space I was aiming. The arrow pierced Henry from side to side.Rafe saw the arrow hit Henry. It unnerved him. He moved closer to Glenn. This was not going the way he had expected it to. It had been easy up until now. None of the other ranches had put up much of a fight. Something wasn't right here.Rafe began to have a bad feeling about this fight. Glenn could smell the sour odor of fear coming from him. It shocked him. It was the first time he had ever seen Rafe afraid.Rafe thought he was hidden in the brush. I saw his outline clearly through it.The arrow came whistling through the brush without any trouble. It caught Rafe in the neck. He was only able to say, "Glenn, he got me," before dying.A shot from a rifle sounded no more than ten feet in front of Glenn. One of the two men left behind him screamed. His companion jumped up to run. I shot him in his back.Glenn had enough. He had lost 13 men and they had not gotten off a single shot. Only he and Grogan were left.Glenn broke. He took off in the direction away from me. He crawled a few yards and then ran swiftly back toward the horses. I was right behind him.Grogan, the last man picked the wrong way to run. He took after Glenn also. The angle he was running and the angle I was running converged.He thought that I was one of them when he first saw me. He almost ran into me. I hit him with the butt of my rifle as I ran past him. It cracked Grogan's skull wide open.The five men on the left side of the cabin heard the shots. They caught a glimpse of Glenn as he jumped on his horse and rode away. They broke and ran also. I got to their horses about the same time they did.I was in the midst of them, shooting my Winchester from the hip. One of them had a shoulder wound. Beth shot him when he stood up to run. It had been a good shot. Only two of the men were able to get on their horses. I shot one of them before he could ride away. One got away.The men who had slipped around to the back of the cabin got into position to fire. The other five went on around to the side, where Jane and Mary were defending.They cut loose at the gun slots in the shuttered windows.I moved toward the rear of the building. Only Glenn and one other man had escaped from the front and left side.Jesse let the five men get past him before he stood up. They were laying down a continuous fire into the windows. Nat had to stay away from the gun slot. An occasional bullet came through the slot and rattled around inside the cabin.Jesse could have killed most of them from ambush. It wasn't his style.He yelled to them, "Look this way and see who's going to send you to hell."The men turned. Jesse waited until they faced him before he pulled his gun. They thought he was still on their side.He killed two of them before he got unlucky. None of the bullets had even come close to him. One of them ricocheted off a rock, hitting the trigger of his gun. It cut off his trigger finger.He switched the gun to his left hand and killed the third man.One of the men stood up from behind his rock so he could shoot Jesse. Nat heard the gunplay outside. Since none of the shots had been fired at the cabin, he stepped up to the gun slot, saw the man about to shoot Jesse. He drilled him through his head. The only man left in the rear got Jesse. He shot him in the chest. It was a freak shot. The man was turning to run, He shot without looking behind him.The bullet broke Jesse's spine after going through his chest. Jesse sat down slowly behind the rock. His gun slipped from his paralyzed fingers. I reached him a second later.Jacobs, the gunman who shot Jesse, was running for his life. He didn't know that he had hit Jesse. He didn't even care. He just wanted to get away from there.I propped

Jesse up. Jesse's face was glowing. He was at peace with himself. All of his anger was gone. He knew he didn't have long to live.He told me, "It's kind of funny. I've looked for death ever since my family was killed. I've fought 30 gunfights, hoping to get killed in each one of them. I won all of them. I have never killed a man that didn't need killing."He continued, "The first time I go against my instincts by listening to Black Jack, I get myself killed. Tom, do me a big favor. Get Black Jack for me. He's the one man who really needs to be killed."He sighed and looked upward, "I'm finally going to see my family again."Blood trickled out of his mouth staining his black coat and white shirt. His head fell over to the side. Jesse had found peace again. He was smiling. He was dead.I went after Jacobs, the man who shot Jesse. He had a good lead. I entered the brush behind him. In his panic Jacobs had left an easy trail for me to read. I could tell by the tracks that Jacobs made that he was scared out of his wits. I could hear Jacobs thrashing wildly in front of him. Then the noise stopped.I felt someone watching me. I looked around carefully. I couldn't see any one. The noise started again in front of me.I continued on after Jacobs. I moved off the trail and circled making no noise.Jacobs stopped behind a sand dune. He knew someone was after him and closing in on him. He planned to ambush whoever came over the dune after him. He had made himself calm down some.I came up behind him. Jacobs was looking back at his trail.I told Jacobs, "This is for Jesse." Jacobs tried to get his gun up. I shot him several times.

Victorio and Nana had been watching the action. I felt their presence.Without turning around I said, "It is good to be near my father and brother again."Victorio grunted his approval as he and Nana walked up behind me. "If my son had let this fool get him, I would have disowned him."Nana chuckled, "My brother is still a good Apache warrior. We were ready to help but you did not need us."

"My father and brother are always welcome to help or watch me kill rats such as these."Victorio and Nana both smiled. Each of them touched their chest as a sign of respect. I returned it. "I have come to see my son for the last time. The Shaman has dreamed of my death, and the death of most of my people. I have had the same dream. It will come true."Victorio had not changed any. "Most of the women and children are on the Fort Stanton Reservation. I have broken out for my last fight. Morning Star has chosen to go with me."I wanted to say to Victorio that he was wrong. Yet deep down in his heart, I knew Victorio was right. He had been living on borrowed time for the past several years.Back at the cabin, five outlaws were preparing to rush the side of the cabin that Jane and Mary were guarding. Jane could see the foot of one of the men hiding in the brush. She shot it. The man rolled over and grabbed his foot. She shot him in the head.Nat slipped out the back of the cabin since it was clear and no more firing was coming from there. He got behind the four men who were still firing at the shuttered window that Jane and Mary were behind.He shot one of the men just as they jumped up to try to run to the side of the cabin. They planned to slide down the wall after they got there and shoot some of the ones in the cabin through the gun slots. They didn't know that most of the rest of the outlaws were dead. The three men kept shooting at the window as they rushed it.Inside Mary let out a small cry. One of the outlaw's bullets had splintered the edge of the shutter. A long thin splinter had hit Mary in her upper arm along with the bullet.The men rushing the cabin quit firing for a second. Jane shot as fast as she could. She killed two of the outlaws and wounded the third one in the leg. It knocked him down. Nat saw the man go down. He shot him again when he tried to get up. The fight was over. No shots were being fired any where around the cabin.Jane didn't know that Mary had been hit until she turned and saw her slumped down in a chair. She rushed over to Mary.Mary was pale and obviously in great pain.Still standing out in the brush with Victorio and Nana, I noticed that the shooting had ended.Beth and Susan had not fired a shot. The men supposed to rush them had never got in position.Victorio smiled at me, "The two men who broke and ran, happened to run right into two of my braves. They will not bother anyone again."I asked them to come with me and meet my real family, and my future wife.Nana didn't want to go and see them, but he came with us. He would not have gone with anyone else but Lone Eagle. Victorio was curious and wanted to see the people who had molded such a great warrior as Lone Eagle.He told me, "We have tried to travel the road of peace with the white eyes and bluecoats several times. We have gone into the Fort Stanton and the San Carlos Reservations. We were told that the past was forgiven and that we could live in honor and peace."

"It was a lie. The white eyes have never kept their word. We heard that civilians were coming to the reservation to hang me. The blue coats would not defend me. The word of the white eyes is written in sand. It does not take a lot of wind to blow it away."Nana looked at me. "The rest of our people are on their way to the mountains of Mexico. We will catch them. It was Victorio's wish to see you for the last time. It is my wish also."Victorio nodded his head. "It is hard to understand the white eyes. They are never satisfied. Sometimes I think that Ussn has decided that all the Apaches should be in the other world where truth and courage will always be honored."I gave the signal that I was coming in. I walked in front of Victorio and Nana so that no one in the cabin would think that I was a hostage or in danger.We walked into the clearing in front of the cabin. Sam almost shot Victorio anyway.Sam told the others. "Stay in the cabin." He walked out of the cabin cradling his rifle in his arms.Nat was still outside. He circled and was watching me and the two Apaches from 60 yards away. He had his rifle pointed at Victorio.Sam walked up to Nana, Victorio and me. He and Victorio locked eyes. Victorio saw no fear in Sam's eyes. Sam saw no anger or danger in Victorio's eyes.Nana said something in Apache to me. "Tell the young man with the rifle to come in also. He might get nervous and shoot one of us."I motioned for Nat to come on in. Each of them kept looking each other over as Nat walked in.Victorio nodded his head. He could see that I came from warrior stock. He had suspected it when I turned out to be such a good fighter.Nana also could see that Sam would be a good friend and a bad enemy. It was the way of warriors.I introduced them to each other. To my surprise, Victorio offered his hand to Sam and then to Nat. Victorio had never done that in front of me. He did this to honor Sam. He had not accepted many ways of the whites. He still felt that he was vulnerable when someone had his hand, especially his right hand.Nana saw Victorio do it and did it also. He shook Sam's hand and then Nat's. He was impressed by both of them. He had to try Nat out. He squeezed down on his hand. Nat returned the pressure ounce for ounce.Nana smiled for the first time. "This is a home of warriors." I interpreted what he said.Victorio told me, "I see only anger in your true father's eyes. That is good. A man who forgives too quickly does not have a strong heart. He might betray you."I saw Jane standing in the doorway of the cabin. She too had a rifle in her hands. She was ready for anything. She was as pale as a ghost. I motioned for her to come over. Beth was right behind her. Susan and Mary followed them. Susan had her arm around her mother. A makeshift bandage had been placed on the arm. Jane had left the splinter in. She didn't want it to break off.I told my mother, "This is Victorio, great Chief of the Chiricahua Mimbre Apaches. He is the one who adopted me."Jane's first impulse was to shoot Victorio, then she realized that I would not be here if it had not been for him. She walked over to him and offered her hand.Victorio was not accustomed to dealing with women. But he looked at her and thought. "It is good. She too is of warrior stock. Morning Star and I can cross over to the other world in peace now. He is a son that will be remembered by both the Apaches and the settlers."Beth was introduced along with Mary and Susan. Victorio looked long and hard into Susan's eyes, when I said, "This is my future wife."Victorio was happy now. He knew Susan and I could have many strong children. He would always have someone to remember him and continue his line. Lone Eagle would tell his sons the story of the Apaches and of Victorio.This woman would bear strong sons to keep his line going. The Apaches saw no difference in adopted sons and true sons.Victorio saw the splinter protruding from

Mary's arm. He asked me to ask Mary if it he could look at it. She nodded. He looked at it and took his knife out. I told Mary, "Don't worry, he has treated many wounds and removed many arrows and bullets."Victorio made a tiny cut. He pinched the arm above the wound. He held the splinter firmly with two fingers and pulled it free. It had gone a couple of inches into her skin.He made another tiny incision and removed the bullet that had not gone deep. It was just under the surface of the skin. The thickness of the shutter had slowed the bullet down so that it had barely penetrated the skin.Mary did not move even an eyelash. Victorio gave her the bullet. He pulled a pouch from around his neck. He put some of the healing herbs on the wounds. He always carried some with him.Nana stood some ten feet from them. He still hated the white eyes. I was the only exception in his hate. He grudgingly admitted to himself, that I had come from good stock. Not as good as Apache but better than most white eyes. Sam had the look of a warrior to him. He probably was wise also. Lone Eagle's mother would make a good Apache wife. Susan and Beth would make good wives also. Mary, the other woman, he had some doubts about. She would probably be bossy.He and Victorio had watched the fight with the outlaws develop. They had been on higher ground than even Lone Eagle was when the fight began. Nana was not surprised that the outlaws fought so poorly. They were short of courage and honesty. He wondered to himself. "How did the white eyes ever get the upper hand over the Apaches?" Nana was glad that the Shaman had forecast the last great battle of the Apaches. He and Victorio were feeling their years. He was tired of the women and children not having enough to eat. Quannah, his son, had already gone to the other world. His wife had made that journey years ago. If it were his time to go, he would take as many enemies with him as he could. I motioned for him to come over. Nana was also introduced. Nana had been looking all of them over. The family of Lone Eagle would not be killed easily. They would take many with them. Nat, the youngest son, was tall and straight. He would make a good enemy or friend. The women would produce strong sons. He might have been interested in one of them for his second wife if it had been possible. It was a good thing the ladies didn't know what he was thinking.I motioned once again for Nana to come over. I told my family what a great warrior and friend Nana was. I didn't tell them that he was a war Chief, or that he was the one who had killed Jesus.It was time for Victorio and Nana to go. Victorio had a date with destiny.Victorio looked at Sam and said in halting English, "Lone Eagle has more Eagle feathers than any Apache has ever earned. He is our greatest Apache. It is because he comes from such a strong family. All of you would have been good Apaches."It was the biggest compliment Victorio could have given them. Niger Lobo (Black Wolf) brought up Victorio"s and Nana's horses. Victorio looked at me. "Stay strong my son, we will meet again in the other world."Victorio and Nana leaped on their horses, clasped their hands to their chests, and they were gone.I walked to the rear of the cabin and picked up Jesse. I told Sam and the others. "Jesse will be buried like the warrior he was. Jesse has gone home."I found a place high in the rocks. I put Jesse and his guns in a crevice. He would still be a warrior in the other world. I piled rocks over him.The 28 dead outlaws were put in Sam's wagon and hauled a couple of miles out in the desert and dumped. The predators would clean up the desert.We had collected all the guns and ammunition from the dead outlaws. Sam had a small arsenal he could use to trade to McGregor the next time he went into Santa Fe. The horses and saddles of the outlaws were put in his corral. He would sell them too.Nat rode over to see how Don Luis had come out with the outlaws. Sam and I stayed at the ranch just in case some of the outlaws came their way. I told Nat to look for the man dressed in black.Nat found Don Luis and his men in the front of the walls of his ranch. Eight men were hanging in the cottonwood trees as he rode in.

Chapter Twenty-One

Don Luis told him what happened. "We were ready when the outlaws got here. All of my men were hid. We opened up on the outlaws when I gave the signal."Black Jack did not ride in with his men. Don Luis could see him and five of his men staying just out of rifle range.The other men came riding in as fast as they could. They swept in through the open double gates. They began firing as they came through them.They rode right up to the home of Don Luis firing as they came. They had thought they would find some men in the courtyard. Two of Don Luis's men had hidden behind the gates. They closed the gates as soon as the last man rode in. The outlaws were trapped. "I gave the signal. Murderous fire from the men hidden on the walls rained down on the trapped men. Fire from all the buildings close to them made the outlaws ride back toward the gates. They couldn't get out."

"The outlaws milled around firing at the walls and the buildings. It was all over in less than five minutes. Dead outlaws lay everywhere. Only two of the outlaws were unharmed. They threw down their guns and raised their hands to surrender. Ten of the 38 men were wounded but still living. Four of them died soon after. One was hard hit but he lived long enough to hang. The others had various kinds of non-lethal wounds."Black Jack sent two of the five men with him to check on the men inside the ranch. They got 100 yards from the walls when they were shot out of the saddle.Black Jack was no fool. He had seen and heard enough to know that it was not his day. He turned and rode away as fast as he could. The three men followed him.Out of the 69 men who began the raid, only he, and the three men with him were left.Don Luis said, "We promptly hung the six wounded, and the two unwounded outlaws. Three of the wounded men begged for mercy. They didn't receive any. All the dead outlaws were taken outside. I told Ramon to take the bodies out into the desert and dump them just as Nat arrived. Nat listened as Don Luis told how the outlaws were killed. He looked the dead outlaws over. None of them were dressed in black.Nat told Don Luis of their fight with the outlaws. Don Luis decided to go back to the Davis cabin with Nat."

Nat didn't tell Don Luis of the visit by Victorio, until they were on their way back.Don Luis had never heard of a visit by Apaches that didn't end in tragedy. He wasn't sure he understood how or why Victorio had come in peace.He left Ramon in charge of his ranch. He wanted to see me and find out the details on Jesus' death. He also wanted to know how I had escaped.Now he also wanted to know more about the visit by Victorio. Maria would not be able to listen to the details. She had never fully gotten over the death of Jesus.Don Luis and Nat didn't get to the ranch of Sam Davis until after dark.Nat gave the signal as they rode in.Nat told me, "I looked all the dead men over. Black Jack is not among them."

Somehow it didn't surprise me. I knew that one day soon Black Jack and I would meet again. It would be settled once and for always. One of us would not be around after that.After Jane had introduced Mary and Susan to Don Luis, she fed them. The others had already eaten. Don Luis was told of my future marriage to Susan.Don Luis couldn't believe I was standing in front of him. In his mind he still pictured me as the little boy that had been captured. He could sense the strength in me. I reminded him of Ramon. Neither of us would ever have to tell anyone that we were good strong fighting men.

Don Luis asked me about Jesus.I told it like it was. Don Luis jerked his head a little when I told how Jesus had been hit with the war club. I didn't tell them that it was Nana who did it. Don Luis would have liked to have some Apaches in front of him right then.His blood surged and he balled up his fists as he listened. I left nothing out except Nana's name.Don Luis asked about my time with the Apaches.Again I told it like it was. I told of how hard it had been until I began to see why the Apaches were the way they were. I told of my adoption and training. I told how Victorio and all of the Apaches had to fight to survive. Finally I told him how I had become one of them.I expressed my feeling that the Apaches were much like the settlers. They were forced to be the way they were.Don Luis listened with mixed emotions. He said nothing. At first he couldn't believe that I had actually become one of the Apaches. How could a white man become friends with the Apaches? They were the ones who had killed his son.It took him a while before he began to think of the Apaches as being something other than savages or animals. It was a disturbing thought. I told him how Victorio made sure everyone was fed and sheltered. It was something that he had never considered before. Finally he asked me. "Do you think that it is possible for the Apaches and us to live in peace?"

"It is possible but I think it is too late. The day of the Apache is over. It might have been possible years ago if the Apaches and the settlers had been able to make even one, lasting, honorable peace between them. None of the Apaches understand the settlers. None of the settlers understand the Apaches. Now they will never do so."It was hard for Don Luis to comprehend. The Apaches and the Mexicans had lived too long by the old law of "An eye for an eye, and a tooth for a tooth." It had always been kill or be killed with them. They had no common ground to build on between them.Don Luis shook my hand. "Maybe something good can come out of what has happened to you and Jesus. You understand both the Apaches and the settlers."He thought, "If we had been able to live together with the Apaches, my son would be alive today."I finished my story and answered the questions that Don Luis asked about Apache life. It was late when we finished talking. We were supposed to leave early the next morning for Santa Fe.Don Luis bought all of the horses left by the dead outlaws from Sam. It would save Sam a trip into Santa Fe. Don Luis told Sam, "We will never have enough horses for my ranch. Some of these horses are no good but most of them will do. Ramon will come over soon and get the horses."

Don Luis mentioned that his ranch needed some supplies from McGregor's in Santa Fe. He also said, "If Tom and the ladies could stay one more day, the ladies could ride into Santa Fe in one of his covered wagons. It would be much more comfortable for Mary."Sam casually asked Jane and Beth if they would like to go in with Mary and Susan and stay a few days with them at the boarding house. It made Beth and Jane's eyes sparkle. Mary told Sam, "There's room for you and Nat also. It'll do you a lot of good."

"Nat and I need to round up the stock and keep an eye on this place. It'll be great for Jane and Beth."It was arranged to meet Ramon and the Rodriquers brothers at the place where the paths to the two ranches came together.Every one went to bed happy. Their life had taken a decided turn for the better.I had one disturbing thought on my mind. "Where was Black Jack?"Black Jack realized that someone had to have betrayed him. It had to be Jesse. His grand scheme to take over the ranches was over. He thought that Jesse might be a little soft when it came to women and children, but he had no idea that Jesse would turn against him.It had to be the fault of Tom Davis. He should have gone into Santa Fe himself, when he heard that Tom had been made the Town Marshall. He and several of his men should have ambushed him. Every time he turned around Tom Davis showed up.It was not too late to do something about it. He thought, "I'm going to kill Jesse too, even though I really like him. Black Jack didn't know that, lucky for him, Jesse was dead. Black Jack and the three gunmen, who were left, rode back to their camp.Black Jack wondered. "How could a man like Jesse be so soft toward women?" He didn't understand it. "All of this was because of the Gilliam woman. Why would Jesse throw everything away because of those two women?" Black Jack had never felt responsible for anyone but himself.Tom Davis had to be involved in this. He had been bad luck for him every time he showed up.He had picked the best men among the outlaws to be his guards.When he saw the buzzards circling and landing just in front of them, he had a bad feeling. They rode into a small clearing. The buzzards debated about staying for a moment before flying off because the men rode up. They circled again and again until the men left. The desert had been good to the buzzards lately.Black Jack caught his breath when he saw who it was. It was Rafe and Waco. They may have both still been alive when the first buzzard had gotten to them. You could tell they had struggled to break free from the stakes that held them. It was obvious that they had been captured and staked out by Apaches. The three men with Black Jack looked around. They were afraid. They mounted their horses and rode on. They didn't want any part of the Apaches. Another large flight of buzzards in the distance told them of the fate of at least one more of Black Jack's men.Black Jack and his three men rode quickly away from the clearing, leaving the bodies of the two men to the buzzards.As they rode back to their hideout, all of them kept looking over their shoulders. Each of them expected to hear the Apache war cry any minute.Black Jack had one more ace up his sleeve. He had been so certain that he was going to take the ranches that he had made arrangements for two more gunmen to join him.Both of them had their name on wanted posters. Seth Gumble was rated right up there with Billy the Kid. Larry Billings wasn't rated at all. He was faster and more dangerous than Seth and Seth knew it and was afraid of him.Seth had been given credit for some of Larry's kills. It didn't bother Larry. He just enjoyed gunning down fast guns. He had his own code of ethics. He never back shot a man. He always killed them on even terms. They always had a chance to draw.They were coming out to meet Black Jack in a few days. He had planned to let them kill Tom and take over as Town Marshal, after he had taken the ranches. At least he could still have them kill Tom. He would rob everybody in Santa Fe and get enough money to start all over again.The next morning Don Luis rode back to his ranch.Susan, Mary and I spent a very enjoyable day with my family. Sam and Nat took me all over the ranch. Sam had rigged a pump in the well and now water flowed out to the corral through terra cotta pipe bought in from Santa Fe. It saved them a lot of time. The corral had been enlarged enough to hold up to 100 steers or horses. It was a working ranch. They could water the livestock with out going outside. Don Luis thought it was a good idea so he did it too.The women had a good time. Susan and Mary spent hours helping Jane and Beth with their hair. They also helped them pack for the trip. Sam had told them to stay as long as they wanted to. It was going to be fun for them. They had not made many trips into Santa Fe for entertainment. The ranch took most of their time. Today was almost like a holiday. It reminded Jane of when they lived back in Georgia.Jane and the other ladies outdid themselves on the supper meal. Steak, enchiladas, tortillas, tamales, beans, potatoes, biscuits and gravy topped off by a wild berry pie. All of them left the table groaning.Jane played the piano and even Sam and I joined briefly in one song "Clementine." All of them went to bed happy and tired. Sam couldn't help but notice that Jane seemed to get younger and younger every day since Tom had come back.The women were ready to go about 9.A.M. the next morning. I wanted to leave earlier than that. I couldn't understand why it took them so long to get ready. Sam had expected it. They were meeting Ramon and Pedro and Juarez Rodriquers sometime around ten o'clock at the place where the trails met. Mary was uncomfortable but not in too much pain. I had put some more medicinal herbs on the splinter wound and the bullet wound. It had not gotten infected.I led out. Nat brought up the rear. They rode slowly so that Mary would not have any more pain than necessary.They had all the guns and ammunition collected from the dead outlaws tied in bags and put on the spare horses and into the wagons, along with the abundant amount of luggage and food the ladies had packed with their clothes.Don Luis told Sam before he left. "If we could depend on the outlaws to continue raiding us, we would have a good business selling their guns and horses." It had brought a chuckle from Sam, but he was still concerned. It was not over yet. That's why he had decided it was best for Jane and Beth to be in town for a while. He didn't know that Black Jack was also going to Santa Fe.The ladies transferred from their horses to the covered wagon driven by Ramon. Nat took the horses back to the ranch. The ladies had become like a family already. They laughed and talked and had a good time all the way into Santa Fe.I stayed out in front of the wagons scouting. Ramon noticed how careful and good at scouting I was. He could see that I knew what he was doing.They stopped for the night about half way in. They were up early the next morning, eating quickly and moving on. They had no trouble on the trip and pulled into Santa Fe about 2 P.M. that afternoon. The ladies had found out most of the things they didn't know about each other, and they had truly enjoyed the trip.I rode down to the jail to see if Cowboy had any trouble while he was gone.The ladies hurried to the boarding house so that they could take a bath and get the trail dust off them.I found Cowboy at the jail. He was a little more fussy than usual. The food at Bert's cafe wasn't half as good as the food at the boarding house. It had been quiet since I had left.None of the saloons and cantinas had any of the gunmen in them. In fact, the owners of the saloons were beginning to fuss because of the drop in business. I made the rounds, winding up in the Palace Saloon.

Chapter Twenty-Two

Bill Taylor was surprised to see me. He thought that Jesse Thomas would have killed me by now. Bill decided that it was time for him to move on and find another town when he saw me come in.Only a few town's people frequented the bar now. Two of the women who had worked there had moved on down the street to the Mexican Cantina where more action went on.I stayed only a minute. I could see that Bill had not been told of the death of most of the outlaws. It wouldn't be long before he got the word. We went back to the boarding house for supper and for Cowboy to meet my family. Susan met them at the door. Cowboy smiled at me. "Boy, you are one lucky man, she's gorgeous and she cooks too." Beth walked out behind Susan. Cowboy stood there with his mouth open. I had never seen Cowboy pale. He was almost in shock. Cowboy had always been a ladies man. He couldn't even talk now. For him it was love at first sight.I introduced Cowboy to Beth. "This is Cowboy. He saved my life a couple of times. You have to watch out for him though, he's dangerous." Jane had walked in and heard the last part of the conversation and saved the day for Cowboy. She walked over to him and hugged his neck. "I would trust this fine looking young man anytime."Cowboy knew she had to be Tom's mother. He could tell where Beth got her good looks. He flushed red all over.Beth had started to hug Cowboy, like her mother did, but changed her mind. She felt a little uncomfortable about hugging him. She offered her hand.Cowboy could feel his hands getting sweaty all over as he shook her hand. When their hands touched, Beth flushed also. She thought to herself, "He is cute, but he's awfully shy."She didn't know that Cowboy had hardly ever been shy in his life until that first minute with Beth.Cowboy would have enjoyed the supper except for one thing. He was in love. He ate very little. Mary asked him if he were sick. He was sick all right. He was sick in love. He couldn't take his eyes off Beth. He was so afraid that I would tell them about his escapade in Nuevo Laredo with Rosita.He didn't have to worry about it. I had caught on. I could see that Beth was smitten with Cowboy also. Her face had stayed flushed all during the meal. She ate very little also.They had two peaceful days. The women had a great time together. Cowboy and Beth got to talk to each other alone for a few minutes each day. Jane caught on and kept an eye on them.Ramon and the Rodriquers brothers had most of their supplies loaded in their wagons and were about ready to go back to Don Luis' ranch. Don Luis had told him to stay longer if I needed them. Jane and Beth were trying to decide if they wanted to ride back with them or stay a couple more days and Cowboy and me take them back.Beth wanted to stay the extra days. Jane wanted to get back to Sam and Nat.Cowboy was the first one to notice the horses tied to the rail at the Palace Saloon. He checked them out. He stepped inside the saloon and looked the five men over. He told me about them. "It's kind of funny. They're gunmen. It's like they are playing a game with us. A game they figure they can win anytime they want to. They left their guns on the saddle but they act like they can do just about what ever they want to. These men are different."

"Let's go over and look at these different, strange gunmen," I teased Cowboy.If there were trouble, it would start the minute I walked into the saloon. I went in the front door at the same time that

Cowboy stepped in the back door. Cowboy had the Scatter Gun ready.These men made Cowboy nervous. They were too self-assured. However, nothing happened. The five men at the table just looked at Cowboy and me. The five men were looking at us as if we were clay targets. They were looking for a weakness in us.I was doing the same to them. Everything you knew about a man would help keep you from getting killed.One of them was left-handed. He was holding his whiskey glass in his left hand. When we came in he switched it to his right hand. Noticing such things kept gunmen alive.Bill Taylor told me their names. The only two I had heard of was Seth Gumble, and Larry Billings.These men were different, for sure. I could feel their confidence oozing out of them. None of them were afraid of me or Cowboy, even with his scattergun. These men had faced death many times and won.Seth was their spokesman. "We've seen what we needed to see. I don't believe he's as tough as we have heard. Next time we come, we'll stay." They got up to leave. I stepped in front of them. "Why wait until next time? Five of you polecats aren't enough?" The five pair of dead eyes didn't even blink. Seth might have flushed a little. He regained his composure. "If it were up to me, I would handle you myself. Right now would be fine with me. I am looking forward to it." I let them pass.I knew that Seth was a dangerous man. The next man in line seemed somewhat more nervous than the others. He had a smile on his face. "I do believe that Seth has underrated you some, but I know that I can take you. Enjoy yourself until we meet again."I knew that Larry Billings was more dangerous than Seth.I watched them as they buckled on their guns. The left-handed man wore two guns. His left gun was tied low on his hip. His right gun was worn higher up. He really was left- handed. I had thought at first that the man might be trying to make me believe he was left handed instead of right handed.One of them wore a shoulder holster. Billy Smith started using it first. It worked for him until he called out Wes Hardin.I figured that three of them were back shooters. One of the back shooters was the left-handed man. Larry and the man with the shoulder holster would fight a fair fight. Seth would be the only fast gun among the back shooters. The other two would be no better than average speed when drawing their gun.Seth would be good and fast. Larry would be faster and better.I would have to kill Larry first, Seth second and then the rest of them.The gunmen were careful not to get their hands too close to their pistols as they rode out.Larry looked back, smiled, and saluted me. Cowboy walked over to where I was. “Did you see that not one of them was worried about me and my scattergun?”

“They are different. They don’t kill for the money. They kill for the pride of being known as the best. It will be a good fight.”

Chapter Twenty-Three

Later on that day Bert Evans brought me a note while I was at the jail. He said, "A lone man left it after eating at my cafe."Cowboy told Bert, "If he ate at your place, we won't have to worry about fighting him. He's already dead." Cowboy laughed as he said this. Bert smiled but he didn't think it was funny.The note read. "You have been responsible for making trouble for me several times. This is the last time. I will meet you on Main Street at high noon tomorrow. I will start from the Barber Shop and you can start from the Boarding House. We will settle this man to man. "It was signed, Black Jack.The note had a P.S. to it. "This will be just between you and me."Cowboy said, "It's a trap. He'll have those five gunmen with him."

"I know it is a trap. We'll have to change his plans and make sure it's one on one."Ramon, Pedro, and Juarez came into the boarding house about that time. "We have heard in the cantina that someone is going to ambush you and kill you tomorrow. We would like to help you."

"Thank you, I will be glad to have you on my side."Cowboy looked at me. "How do you think he will do this?"Bert Evans slipped out while Tom, Cowboy, Ramon and his men were talking. In a few minutes he came back with Zeke and McGregor. "We're in this too. We're not going back to the way it was."I had been thinking. "They will have to slip in and get in position to shoot Cowboy and me. They'll try to slip in early tomorrow morning and hide out until the fight. We'll get there before they do."Ramon said. "We'll be on the street and behind the buildings before it gets light in the morning."Jake told them "We'll be there."I responded, "With you fellows fighting with me, we could beat the United States Army."Ramon, Pedro, and Juarez were offered rooms in the boarding house. They preferred going back to their own rooms. They had a lot of time before the sun came up the next day.They met at the boarding house a long time before dawn. Mary, Jane, Beth and Susan had cooked a big breakfast for them by the time they got there. None of the women had slept much at all. They were worried about me.I had slept soundly. So had Cowboy and all the others. Danger had always been part of our lives.I had always figured that Bill the owner of the Palace Saloon was part of the trouble.

I told Ramon and his men to take the back of the saloon. That was one place some of the men were sure to come. Zeke, Bert and McGregor would check the other buildings. Cowboy and I would make the rounds. If anyone saw or heard anything they would let the others know by three shots in the air.Sure enough two of the gunmen rode up to the back of the Palace Saloon. They were in the middle of dismounting when Ramon and the Rodriquers brothers stepped out from the side of the building.Chad Donehoo was 21 years old. He had killed his first man when he was 16. He had found out he had some talent with a pistol. He didn't have anything else so he used his talent to get respect and money. He had killed 12 more since then.Edgar Chandler was 35. He had drifted all his life. He only fought when the odds were in his favor. He had killed 19 men. Not all of them were fair fights.He took one look at Ramon and the Rodriguers brothers and decided he didn't like the odds. Chad was different. He was kind of fiery.Ramon was ready. "I have heard that you two are mucho malo. You can prove it, or you can unbuckle your gun belts and drop them."

He grinned as he said this.Chad had the wild urge to draw and see if he could beat them. Edgar knew better. "Don't do it, we don't have a chance."He could tell that Chad was going to try. He would get both of them killed. Edgar dove off his horse and grabbed Chad just as he had started to draw. They fell off the horse and Edgar landed on top of Chad.Ramon had already drawn his pistol when he saw Chad's shoulder move. He didn't shoot.Chad had the breath knocked out of him but it saved his life. Edgar wasn't worried about Chad. He didn't want to get killed because of him.Edgar lifted Chad's gun from his holster with two fingers and dropped it on the ground. He did the same with his own.Chad was spitting mad. "I'll kill you when this is all over." Edgar looked Chad over in disgust, "Why you stupid punk, you're nothing but a dumb kid. I can beat you seven days a week. These men would have killed you before you touched your gun. If they let us live, you had better find you a different job. I don't want nothing else to do with you after this." We locked them up.I walked over to the Palace Saloon during the middle of the morning. I told Bill, "I know that you are part of this. When I kill Black Jack, I'm coming back to see you." "What if you don't kill Black Jack? What if he gets you?"

"If Black Jack kills me, Cowboy is coming in to see you. Either way you're going to be dead. I wouldn't wait around until the end of the fight if I were you."Bill thought about it a second. He cleaned out his safe. He went down to the stable, got his horse and rode out of town. He left the saloon open. Black Jack owned it anyway.Cowboy and Tom were told that Ramon had captured two of the outlaws. Where were the other three? Time passed slowly but it was almost time for the fight to begin.The other outlaws didn't show up. I knew they would be here for the final fight between Black Jack and me. Black Jack was no fool. He wouldn't take the chance on a fair fight.

It was two minutes to twelve when Black Jack rode into town. He dismounted at the Barber Shop. We had about 200 yards between us. He and I started walking toward each other at the same time.Cowboy was looking across the street at the saloon when he saw a shadow cross in front of one of the upstairs window. He knew where at least one gunman was.He had his Scatter Gun with him. He ran over to the saloon where men were helping themselves to the whiskey since there was no one to pay. He took the stairs two at a time. He ran to the end of the hall and snatched the door open.Bob Gentry was raising his rifle to shoot me in the back when Cowboy got there. The door was opened so violently that it slammed against the wall. Bob spun around with his rifle.Cowboy shot both barrels of the shotgun at the same time.It blew Bob right through the window. The rifle hit the floor as Bob flew out the window. He landed spread eagled, a crumpled, bloody heap in the dusty street below. The cloud of dust that came up when he hit the street flew away as quickly as his soul did.Cowboy picked up the rifle Bob Gentry had dropped. He kept watch on the street below him. Every one but Black Jack and me had ducked behind the buildings when they heard the shots. His shots almost started the fight although Black Jack and I were still too far apart for pistols to be accurate. We still had fifty yards to go.Cowboy saw Seth Gumble step out from the empty building he had spent the night in. Seth had his rifle ready. Cowboy shot him with the rifle Bob Gentry had dropped.I saw Larry Billings step out from the women's dress shop. He too had spent the night there. The owner of the shop lay tied up in the back room. Two customers that had come in that morning were tied up with her. Larry was almost shaking in his eagerness to begin the fight. The gunmen had been smart enough to know that they would be expected to try and slip in town the next morning. They had come in the night before. I didn't know if Larry was going to wait for Black Jack or if he was going to start the action. I figured he would wait since he was not one to take advantage over his enemy.Cowboy couldn't see Larry since he was standing under a porch. I knew I would have to face the two of them at one time.Larry nodded his head at me as he stepped out on the sidewalk. He and Black Jack were still some 35 yards apart. In a few more steps he and Black Jack would be close enough to draw and shoot. I still figured that Larry was the most dangerous. When Black

Jack and I were still 15 yards apart Black Jack went for his gun. Larry thought Black Jack would get a few yards closer. Larry went for his gun a split second later. The split second was the difference.My bullet caught Larry in the chest. It made him jerk a little. Larry's shot was a little high. It knocked my hat off. Black Jack got one shot off just as I fired at him. I was hit in the left shoulder. My bullet hit Black Jack in the chest. Black Jack raised up on his toes some but it didn't knock him down. He shot again. It grazed my right leg. Blood ran freely. I shot him in the chest again. Both of us kept walking toward each other firing as we came. I hit Black Jack in the stomach and in the shoulder. Black Jack's last shot was wild.My last bullet hit Black Jack in the face. Black Jack was a lot of bad things. He certainly was not a coward.Larry Billings had been critically hit. The bullet had knocked him over backwards. It had been close to his heart. He had kept from dying only because of his desire to get one more shot at me. He used all the energy he had left to pull himself up by the post that held the cover over the sidewalk. It was all he could do to point the gun at me.I heard Susan scream. I was beginning to feel weak from the loss of blood. I knew I was out of bullets. I knew that I was about to die. Larry would not miss from that distance. Larry Billings started to tell me, "I knew I could kill you." Susan's shot rang out. Zeke and McGregor both shot Larry. They shot at the same time. A look of surprise crossed Larry's face as he died. Susan had shot him with the rifle she had brought out with her so that she could help me if I needed it. She was that kind of girl. She stood up for her man. Zeke and McGregor also stood up for what they believed. Each of them thought their shot had been the one that killed Larry Billings. It was over. Black Jack and almost all of his men were dead. I turned and walked slowly back toward the boarding house. I only made a few steps before my leg collapsed under me from the loss of blood. I woke up seven hours later in Susan's bed.Jane, Beth, Mary, Susan, Cowboy, Zeke, Jake, Ramon, and half the town were in the room with me. Jane made all of them leave.The bullet in my shoulder had bounced off the bone. It had cracked it but it didn't splinter. It was the worse wound I had. The bullet that grazed my leg had not hit any thing major. I had lost some blood but other than that I was all right. They made me drink lots of water. I was up and walking with a limp the third day. My left shoulder ached, and my leg was sore. I used my herbs on my wounds so I didn't come down with fever. The wounds had been clean. Whiskey had been poured on and into them. My wounds extended the stay of Jane and Beth for a couple of days. Cowboy hated to see me hurt but he asked me. "Can't you stay in bed just a few more days?"He was enjoying his time with Beth. Jane had seen all the signs. She knew that it could get serious very quickly. Beth was 18. She was old enough to make up her own mind, but she had no experience with young men courting her. Jane would have liked for Beth to know a few more young men before getting serious.Jane and Beth had to go home. I promised to come out as soon as I could. Cowboy took Jane and Beth back to the ranch. I stayed the Town Marshall a while longer. Susan and I made plans to get married. Ron Jedrokoski does show up again in my life, and Cowboy and Beth -but that's a part of another story.I didn't tell any one that I had a vision about Victorio while I was unconscious. The day of the gunfight and the vision was October the 20th, 1879. It was one year later on Tres Castilles Mountain on October 20th, 1880, that Victorio was killed in the Candalaria Mountains of Mexico.The vision was so real that I knew it would really happen. It did! Victorio, Morning Star, White Fawn, Chato, White Killer, and Quannah would all be gone to the other world. Only Nana would be left. He was off raiding for food and ammunition when Victorio was killed. I knew that Victorio would go down fighting. He would die a warrior's death. He would die happy. It was the Apache way!

Epilogue

The Death Of Victorio After Tom left, Victorio tries to make peace with the white eyes. They had promised him his Apaches could remain on the "Mescalero Reservation" and not be sent to "San Carlos" where there was nothing but Sage Brush and sand. They broke their word. They were sent to San Carlos. They also promised that Victorio and his Apaches would be given amnesty for all the raids and killings committed by them in the past.Some one who had lost a loved one during an Apache raid got a warrant for Victorio's arrest. Information came to Victorio on the Reservation that they were going to hang him and many of his warriors after the trial.Victorio talked to the Commanding Officer of the Calvary Troop next to the Reservation and was told. "This it is a civilian affair, the Army can not get involved." The Indian Agent would not get involved. The Military was going to let them hang him. Victorio's source of information, a warrior on the Reservation, got word to him. The Indian agent knew about it. He didn't tell Victorio about it. That night Victorio and fifty of his braves killed eight troopers and stole all the horses and many guns and ammunition from the 9th Calvary. Victorio was on the run again. He had to leave the Reservation with the few remaining warriors he had left.All of the next year Victorio kept the Armies of Mexico and the United States busy. Finally The United States and Mexico agreed to let each other's Army cross the border any time they were chasing Victorio and/or his Apaches.Victorio had Comanche, Navajo, Cheyenne and others joining him in his final fight against the white eyes. All the Indians in the Indian Nations were being killed or brought into the Reservations one by one. All of them would eventually lose their freedom. Geronimo, Juh, and Cabelleros joined him.Victorio fought up and down both sides of the border. Lozen his sister, one of the women warriors, had a sixth sense. She could tell which direction the soldiers were coming from. Because of this Victorio could run or ambush them. He won every skirmish but he lost men every time he had to fight. He couldn't afford to lose them.The newspapers were hard on the Army. Headlines read, "Fifty Apaches Keep 5000 Soldiers busy chasing them but not catching them."The President ordered General William T. Sherman, "The Federal Hero of Atlanta" to bring an end to Victorio and his Apaches. In "The War Between The States," Sherman had burned Atlanta and a 20 mile-wide strip of land from Atlanta to Savannah. It was about 300 miles long. General Crook was brought in too.General Crook got Geronimo to surrender with the help of Lt. Gatewood, Tom Jeffords and his Apache Scouts.Victorio stayed out of the Reservations. He had to change camps every time the Armies came after him. His Apaches would run back into the Northern Mountains of Mexico where the American Army couldn't go. The Mexican and the American Armies kept him on the move all the time. Another fighting force came on the scene.

Three hundred Mexican veterans under an old Indian fighter found the trail of Victorio and forced him to make a fatal mistake. Maybe he was tired of running. Maybe Ussen told him to stop and fight. Whatever the reason Victorio picked a place to fight in they couldn't retreat from. They climbed about half way up the middle peak of the Three Castilles Mountains in Mexico. Victorio and his Apaches were almost out of food and ammo. They had already run out of water. The

Mexicans had plenty of food, water and supplies.

They had fought a couple of hours on the 19th of October. Victorio knew it was over. It would be a fight to the death. It was the morning of the 20th. Victorio had his body between Morning Star and the boulder they had used to hide behind in yesterday's battle. Victorio's spirit was resting in the world between sleep and being awake. The sun began its daily trek across the sky. The first rays of the sun hit his feet that were protruding from behind the boulder. He pulled his legs up tighter against Morning Star to protect her. The boulder they were behind was not very large. He woke up instantly ready to finish the fight he had known was coming. He knew this was their last day on earth.

The Mexicans took their time. They finished breakfast and started the final rush against the Apaches. The Apaches let them get close since they were almost out of ammunition. The Mexicans kept coming. They commenced firing at the Apaches that were left. They couldn't see Victory but they knew where he was. They shot bullet after bullet into the rocks behind him.

Victorio had known this day was coming for years. So had Lone Eagle, Morning Star and the Shaman. It was good that his son Lone Eagle did not have to travel his path to the other world today.

Victorio told the older warriors, children and women, "Hold up your hands, walk down the path and surrender." The Mexicans gathered them in and sent them on down the mountain under guard. The Mexicans were not in a hurry. They kept coming up the peak. The Apaches were hungry, thirsty and almost out of ammunition and arrows. The time for the dying had begun. Every time a shot came from an Apache behind a rock, ten shots answered. The bullets ricocheted all around the Apache until one hit him. The Mexicans continued their climb up the peak. Victorio and Morning Star were trapped like the other Apaches. The Mexicans kept on coming. They killed every warrior that resisted. Victorio touched Morning Star's hand and held it for a moment. A bullet bounced off the rocks behind them and slammed into her back. One sigh and she was gone. Victorio was hit two times before a ricocheting bullet hit him in the head killing him. The Mexican force captured all the Apaches that surrendered and killed the ones who resisted. They killed all the warriors. Some of the women and young children were given as slaves to some of the wealthier Mexican families. They used them as domestic laborers.

The death of Victorio and Morning Star happened just like the Lone Eagle's dream had predicted.

Rumors were started that Victorio had shot Morning Star and then himself. It was not true. Every living Apache knew it was a lie.

Nana was off on a raid and was not killed. Nana and Geronimo leave the reservation again and fight for a few more years but the Apaches are no longer a nation large enough to give the U.S. Army much trouble. Victorio and Morning Star have been killed just like Tom's vision from Ussn . Later on a Mexican is killed in an Apache raid on his small village. He has Victorio's bridle and reins on his horse. He was lucky they killed him before they found he had the reins and bridle.

Tom is able to go back to being town Marshall. Cowboy remains his deputy. He spends about half his time at Sam Davis' ranch. Tom and Susan get married. So do Cowboy and Beth. Mary decides to go back home to Virginia. Sam and Jane stay where they are. Sam tells everyone that Jane wouldn't move to any other place. Neither would he. Santa Fe remains the mid point of the pioneer's trek across America. Cowboy and Tom share other adventures when they decide to join the pioneers on their way to California. Tom meets Jedrokoski again. That's another story, yet to be told.